flambeau

Version
2.0

flambeau

Version 2.0

---

don hawkins

Kregel
Publications

flambeau 2.0

© 2002 by Don Hawkins

Published by Kregel Publications, P.O. Box 2607, Grand Rapids, MI 49501.

For more information about Kregel Publications, visit our Web site: www.kregel.com.

Scripture quotations are from *The New King James Version.* © 1979, 1980, 1982, Thomas Nelson, Inc., Publishers.

Library of Congress Cataloging-in-Publication Data
Hawkins, Don.
   Flambeau 2.0 / by Don Hawkins.
      p.   cm.
    1. Demonology—Fiction. I. Title: Flambeau two.zero.
II. Title.

PS3558.A8229 F59   2002
813'.6—dc21
2002006248

ISBN 0-8254-2874-2

Printed in the United States of America

02 03 04 05 06 / 3 2 1

Acknowledgments

Every book, even if written by a single author, is the product of the efforts of many people. I would like to express my gratitude and appreciation to those who have contributed to this new Flambeau project.

To my wife, Kathy, for extraordinary encouragement and input on the concepts

To Dawn Leuschen for typing and retyping the manuscript

To Allen Bean for editorial expertise and content input

To Warren Wiersbe for sage wisdom and encouragement

To Dennis Hillman and the team at Kregel for significant efforts to bring this work to reality, including Paul Ingram's editorial revisions and Sarah De Mey's diligence.

Finally, to all those who gave so much positive feedback on *flambeau@darkcorp.com*, which motivated me to continue writing in this genre.

Don Hawkins

Introduction

When you do something different, you run a risk. Your work may be viewed as innovative, or it may be written off as some quirky attempt at humorous or avante-garde communication.

Without question, *flambeau@darkcorp.com*, the predecessor to this book, was identified by many who read it as "different." Like *The Screwtape Letters*, a provocative C. S. Lewis approach to understanding Christian discipleship by imagining how the demons might view it, *flambeau@darkcorp.com* sought to view spiritual concepts related to the local Christian congregation from the same perspective. Lewis referred to this reverse perspective as "moral inversion," the deliberate reversal of the holy and the unholy, where lies are spoken as if they are true and truth is treated as a lie. This book is similar in format, though it looks at somewhat different issues.

I've been encouraged with the responses of readers who view this as a creative way to look at some serious spiritual issues and dangers. As one pastor said, "*flambeau@darkcorp.com* is the most innovative approach to Satan's strategies I've seen since *Screwtape Letters*." Another reader, an active layman, said, "I think you shed light on how Satan uses such things as criticism, intimidation and seduction to undermine faith—and the motif of counterfeit spiritual gifts is both plausible and consistent with Satan's character as a counterfeiter."

I was gratified to learn that I am not the only author who believes Lewis's approach still has the power to communicate. At the 1999 Christian Booksellers Association convention, my wife and I were having dinner with a Christian publisher who told me that he knew of at least two other books using a *Screwtape*-type motif that were in process for 2000 lists. Since our publication came out in 1999, we wound up being the "first on the block." Rather than as competition, I regarded company on the bookstore shelves as confirmation that this is a worthwhile approach.

There are significant differences between *flambeau 2.0* and its predecessor. The original *flambeau@darkcorp.com* focused on the area of spiritual gifts, pointing out how Satan might seek to disrupt a local body of believers by counterfeiting these gifts—introducing opposition, discouragement, and sarcasm in place of encouraging, teaching, and serving. *Flambeau 2.0* looks at the apostle Paul's references to Satan's strategies of spiritual warfare in the crucial but sometimes underappreciated 2 Corinthians. Paul's ministry had come under the intense attack of those who wished to discredit his calling and service as an apostle. This letter has a great deal to say about encouragement, suffering, and perseverance, but we will look specifically at Paul's references to Satan's "devices," to use his term in 2:11.

To prepare for victory, we must know our enemy's strategy. Satan is presented in Scripture as the ultimate adversary of our God and the great enemy of the faith. Yet many Christians still think of the Devil in Halloween caricature—dressed up in red flannel, holding a pitchfork, his face frozen in a stupid leer. This does not fit reality, but how happy Satan must be when Christians fail to take his methods seriously.

In 2 Corinthians, Satan was after the apostle Paul. He was motivating his followers to hinder the apostle's work. With these attacks weighing heavily on his mind, Paul includes six specific references to Satan in this Epistle. I've been especially challenged to develop these references in speaking to churches and in ministry to missionaries. God has used these insights to such an extent that I felt a book on the subject would be helpful.

My major thesis is this:

Satan, the primary deceiver and adversary, will seek to sidetrack believers from whatever God wants them to be or do in their lives. To achieve this, he employs certain "devices," which include:

- Producing a lack of love and forgiveness to divide the brethren (2:11)
- Blinding lost individuals to whom believers are witnessing (4:3–4)
- Prompting Christians to "yoke" or link up with unbelievers (6:11–14)
- Waging war against believers' minds or thought lives (10:3–6)
- Causing false doctrine to sound like God's truth (11:1–4, 13–15)
- Discouraging and intimidating believers through the use of pain and adversity (12:7–10)

Flambeau 2.0 provides a "reverse-perspective" exposition of these six satanic strategies. Readers should be able to spot these "devices," which hinder our spiritual development today. Like its predecessor, this book builds on the concept of the satanic kingdom as a modern multinational corporation, with Satan's corrupted ethics and a total lack of compassion. With Satan as CEO, such a corporation was described in *flambeau@darkcorp.com* (p. 6) as staffed by "status-conscious (but conscience-deficient) demons with cutthroat efficiency."

In *flambeau 2.0*, Flambeau, an ambitious but less than spectacularly successful demon, continues to labor in his assigned field of responsibility, a local church (in Darkcorp's lexicon, "a local competition unit" or "LCU"). Flambeau's general assignment is to subvert Glencrest Bible Church, and his specific responsibility is the neutralization—or, if possible, the reclamation—of Gene, a recent recruit of the Competition. A former marine, Gene has committed his life to Christ (the Competition) after receiving a copy of the Bible (the Competition's Business Plan) from a marine buddy.

In *flambeau@darkcorp.com*, Scraptus, Flambeau's supervisor, writes a series of confidential memos, which come to serve as a manual for counterfeit spiritual gifts. However, because of the relative lack of success of the demons who report to him, including Flambeau, Scraptus finds himself demoted and banished to the Siberian field office. Hotspur, an ambitious sociopathic rival, leapfrogs past Flambeau to take over Scraptus's position, gleefully documenting Flambeau's ineffectiveness in his efforts to regain control over his client Gene or to influence Glencrest.

Now Hotspur demands an "upgrade" in strategy. Their new initiatives develop in e-mail communiqués between the two demons, using 2 Corinthians as a tactical tool for use in improving Flambeau's success rating at Glencrest.

I hope *flambeau 2.0* will remind each reader of the importance of being aware of Satan's strategies. In 1 Peter 5:8–9a, the apostle Peter reminds his readers:

> Be sober, be vigilant; because your adversary the devil walks about like a roaring lion, seeking whom he may devour. Resist him, steadfast in the faith.

Just as an individual taking an evening jog through Central Park in New York City must be alert to the danger posed by muggers, believers must watch out for the enemy of our souls. It would be prudent to follow the advice of Joe Lewis, former heavyweight boxing champion of the world. Over a decade and a half, Lewis was called upon to defend his title twenty-five times. When Bill Stern, the voice of American sports on radio, asked the Brown Bomber how he could have been so successful in such a demanding sport, Lewis replied, "I study my opponent; I plan my fight very carefully. The results are always the same: I'm never surprised and I stay on the offensive." That's exactly how we should treat our adversary the Devil.

I also hope that this book will remind us of the importance of the armor of God described by Paul in Ephesians 6:10–18:

> Finally, my brethren, be strong in the Lord and in the power of His might.
>
> Put on the whole armor of God, that you may be able to stand against the wiles of the devil.
>
> For we do not wrestle against flesh and blood, but against principalities, against powers, against the rulers of the darkness of this age, against spiritual hosts of wickedness in the heavenly places.
>
> Therefore take up the whole armor of God, that you may be able to withstand in the evil day, and having done all, to stand.
>
> Stand therefore, having girded your waist with truth, having put on the breastplate of righteousness, and having shod your feet with the preparation of the gospel of peace; above all, taking the shield of faith with which you will be able to quench all the fiery darts of the wicked one. And take the helmet of salvation, and the sword of the Spirit, which is the word of God; praying always with all prayer and supplication in the Spirit, being watchful to this end with all perseverance and supplication for all the saints.

The apostle Paul understood that watchfulness demands skill in the weapons at hand. When a young man or woman becomes a member of a nation's armed forces, he or she enters some form of basic training. One objective of basic training is to increase physical strength and stamina. No newly enlisted man or woman enjoys calisthenics, forced marches, or grueling obstacle courses, yet these turn flabby recruits into robust soldiers who can keep going under grueling battlefield conditions.

Basic training also qualifies the new soldiers to correctly handle their gear and weapons. Thus armed and strengthened, each soldier is prepared to handle whatever he or she is called upon to face. So it is with us as believers. Weapons are available, strength has been provided—we must simply use them skillfully in the spiritual conflict.

Finally, it is my fervent hope that *flambeau 2.0* will provide believers with a strong, vivid reminder that our victory over the enemy has been secured. As Paul wrote in 2 Corinthians 2:14:

> Now thanks be to God who always leads us in triumph in Christ, and through us diffuses the fragrance of His knowledge in every place.

Paul wanted Corinthian believers to know that Satan has been defeated. Eternal triumph has been secured, and victory is ours to enjoy and experience today. John reminded those who read his book of the Revelation of the reality of this victory and how it can be secured when he wrote in Revelation 12:7–12:

> And war broke out in heaven: Michael and his angels fought against the dragon; and the dragon and his angels fought, but they did not prevail, nor was a place found for them in heaven any longer.
>
> So the great dragon was cast out, that serpent of old, called the Devil and Satan, who deceives the whole world; he was cast to the earth, and his angels were cast out with him.

Then I heard a loud voice saying in heaven, "Now salvation, and strength, and the kingdom of our God, and the power of His Christ have come, for the accuser of our brethren, who accused them before our God day and night, has been cast down.

"And they overcame him by the blood of the Lamb and by the word of their testimony, and they did not love their lives to the death.

"Therefore rejoice, O heavens, and you who dwell in them! Woe to the inhabitants of the earth and the sea! For the devil has come down to you, having great wrath, because he knows that he has a short time."

The message of the loud voice from heaven carries great significance for those claiming God's ultimate victory over the "accuser of our brethren."

In verse eleven, the aged apostle identifies three keys to spiritual victory over the enemy today:

The first key is the blood of the Lamb—there is no victory over Satan apart from Jesus' death on the cross. His shed blood is the ultimate evidence and means of victory.

The second key is the word of their testimony. This phrase could be taken as either the words they testified or the Word to which they gave witness. Based on the identification of the Word of God as the Sword of the Spirit in Ephesians 6:17, I prefer to take the phrase "the word of their testimony" as a reference to the Word of God. Jesus provided us with the ultimate example of how to apply Scripture to gain victory in a series of confrontations with Satan, which are recorded in Matthew 4. Three times He responded to the enemy's assaults with "It is written. . . ."

The third key is that "they did not love their lives to the death." As a one-time participant in football and basketball who had more desire than skill, I learned the importance of giving one-hundred-percent effort. Wholehearted effort can often secure victory over teams with superior skills. My coaches, Rudolph Davidson in high school and Art Philips in college, underscored this lesson often. Anyone who is a sports fan can likely recall a game where a team with less talent and more desire defeated a superior but less motivated opponent. These saints defeated Satan because they were totally committed to the Lord, not to their own self-interest. Such commitment in our walk with the Lord can help secure victory for us today.

I pray that readers of *flambeau 2.0* will keep in mind the desperate need for serious vigilance, for the ability to use our spiritual weapons, and for the appreciation that victory is ours. The fruits of conquest are available to those whose lives are secured by the blood, fortified by the Word, and motivated by commitment to the Lord.

flambeau

Version
2.0

Hotspur Memorandum One

To: flambeau@darkcorp.com
From: hotspur@darkcorp.com
Subject: It's time to get serious

To date, I have not received your strategic plan update, covering your assigned client, Gene, and his local competition unit, Glencrest Bible Church.

As was made clear in my previous memo, your former supervisor, Scraptus, is now cooling his horns at our Siberian field office. There we hope he will learn to more effectively and faithfully serve His Diabolical Majesty.

That brings us to you.

Do not think for a moment that I also will disappear, my dear, incompetent, little demonic trainee. You are all mine for a very long time to come. Not that I yet know what I will do with you. Your work to date has been less than despicable, even for a novice tempter. By the time of your next six-month devaluation, I expect significant changes. You have achieved few results for His Debased Eminence. We can afford no such slackers at this point in our corporate growth strategy.

Your job is to render Gene an ineffective follower of our Chief Competitor's Son and to prepare for a corporate takeover at Glencrest LCU.

Just how do you intend to do it?

Hotspur Memorandum Two

To: flambeau@darkcorp.com
From: hotspur@darkcorp.com
Subject: The Competition's ridiculous strategy

One reason you have failed to craft a strategic takeover strategy seems to be a poor understanding of our Debased Leader's basic objectives. You do not know how to initiate a diversified approach. I intend to correct this glaring deficiency by assigning for your study a document in which our strategic initiatives are spelled out in detail.

Even allowing for the inferior direction you received from Scraptus, there's no excuse for failure. Once you know something about the weaknesses of your clients, they are pliable—even when they do not, strictly speaking, belong to us. When they associate in local competition units, you can mix their weaknesses in delightfully volatile formulas.

All you need is a basic course in human sin chemistry.

You may be surprised at the source I'm recommending for your study. It's the section of the Competition's Business Plan (or BP, their "Bible") that they refer to as 2 Corinthians.

This brief little missive is sickening reading. Their first vice president for European expansion, a character named Paul, spends most of his ink carping and whining about these ungrateful and incompetent wretches at Corinth. We had made some diabolical progress in the Corinth LCU. It was our first sustained attack on the Competition's new expansion efforts using the very people He had gathered at Corinth.

We'd anticipated that these new units would be strongly fortified centers manned by combat specialists who were carefully indoctrinated in our enemy's plan. How delighted we were to find that these cells were hardly fortified at all. The humans in them were recent defectors from our camp. Some were still our people who had just wandered across the line out of curiosity. Some of our fine agents had slipped unnoticed into this poor excuse for a business enterprise.

No wonder Paul was at tender hooks with this crew. His Boss had stuck him with the impossible assignment of whipping them into shape. The first point to burn into your thinking, Flambeau, is that our Opposition's strategy relies on just such ridiculous resources.

Why? No one down here can figure it out. Occasionally their weaknesses and strengths come together to cause trouble, but only after an immense and inefficient effort has been expended in intense remedial training. At times I pity the Competition. Their CEO put together a most surprising invasion in His Son. We spend most of our time now countering this setback. But then He waits until after the big assault before even beginning to gather a second-wave invasion force. The army He assembles is composed of society's washouts, like your Gene.

I know that some of our strategists stalk around with a defeated air. Don't believe it for a second. Unless the opposition comes up with something better than this feeble incursion onto earth and this LCU strategy, His day is done.

You will see.

Hotspur Memorandum Three

To: flambeau@darkcorp.com
From: hotspur@darkcorp.com
Subject: Those wonderful Corinthians

As soon as I sent off the last note, it struck me that you might need background information to help you get the most out of applying 2 Corinthians to your project with Gene and Glencrest Local competition unit.

Soon after our debacle with the CEO's Son, the Competition made a foolishly courageous blunder, placing one of their first bases in the heart of a secure stronghold of our empire. Corinth was a relatively new city. It was colonized by the Roman Empire to control a key shipping point for products into and out of Greece.

Ports are always ideal for our purposes, because there's money to be made, and many of the people are far from their homes and free from old moral constraints. The Corinthians made a name for themselves around the world for their greed, carousing, and sexual habits.

Since people from various human societies gathered there, Corinthians were always finding some reason for becoming angry with one another. Nobody, not even our Competition, was going to keep these hot heads walking in the same direction.

Still, their vice president for European affairs spent eighteen months in his hopeless mission to this city. Don't forget to read the record of his time there in Acts 18:1–18 of their Business Plan. Later he returned for another three months (Acts 20:3 BP). He actually wrote one of his most damaging reports, the book of Romans in the Business Plan, from there. He used Corinth to develop several aspects of the corporate strategy.

Why Corinth? Insanity is one guess. Of course, it was a strategic location from which the Business Plan could be disseminated to far-off places. But Paul told these people that they had been picked for this LCU because they were some of the weakest people that could be found. Do you see why I wonder if there is not some insanity at work on the other side? Near the beginning of the first letter to Corinth (1:22–31 BP) Paul actually told them that the Jewish culture was looking for miracles and the Greeks wanted wisdom. He had neither to offer them. Their CEO had chosen weak and foolish people to believe weak and foolish words that would shame the strong and wise. Then no one could say that anyone had pulled off this victory except the CEO.

Don't try to understand such rot. It is incomprehensible. But remember it, because that's how they put together their LCUs to this day.

Since they threw open the door for anyone who wanted to come in, we could hardly fail to insert our agents and agenda. Those Corinthian clients were geniuses at one thing—getting into trouble. It goes without saying that we threw every kind of temptation in the game book at them. One especially successful ploy was to maximize their tension between what they were *free to do* and what they *ought to do*. They also were open to squabbles about which of them could put on the most spectacular supernatural show. They mumbled around in so many made-up languages that it was impossible to hear any part of the Business Plan in their meetings. So our comedy gag writing team filled the gaps in their thinking with absurd notions about what the CEO was saying.

A lot of the clients in the LCU simply despised each other. They would take one another to court at the slightest offense.

Paul wanted "weak and foolish." He got as much of it at Corinth as he could stomach. We couldn't have put together a better mix of misfits than they did. No wonder Paul wrote such strong words to them.

Flambeau Memorandum One

To: hotspur@darkcorp.com
From: flambeau@darkcorp.com
Subject: Re: Corinthians

In response to your rather strange instruction, I have completed my initial research on the project you ordered—to identify the strategic initiatives of His Debased Majesty that are revealed by the Competition's vice president in 2 Corinthians. I intend to report my findings to you in sections, so that you can review my work and give more examples of your always insightful commentary.

First some general thoughts.

Though placement of an LCU at Corinth turned out to be a significant blunder for the Competition, this Paul does seem to have penetrated our councils. He knew more than he should have been allowed to learn about the strategies he discusses.

I am not quite so uninformed about the setting of this letter as you suppose. It is, after all, a classic case history that all beginning demons study. Obviously our agents successfully penetrated this LCU's defenses—as they never tire of reminding us.

To add background, I went back to refresh my memory about the portion of the Business Plan referred to as 1 Corinthians. There I noted several qualities that could apply in our franchise establishment at Glencrest and other LCUs today.

They are as follows:

- Major divisions and contentions. Some claim allegiance to Paul, others to one of the other executives, or even to the CEO's Son alone (1 Cor. 1:10–12 BP). They fight about how far to emphasize a ritual involving water. Some seem to think that this "baptism" should have the same status as the core message (1 Cor. 1:14–17 BP).

- An emphasis on sophisticated human wisdom (1 Cor. 1:18–30 BP).
- A desire to keep a foot in our world (1 Cor. 3:1 BP).
- A nonconfrontational, relaxed view of actions that are not allowed in their Business Plan. They are even willing to go further in these actions than is considered acceptable by our own people (1 Cor. 5:1 BP).
- A tendency to turn even the smallest of conflicts with each other into major cases that have to be settled in secular courts (1 Cor. 6:1 BP).
- An arrogance regarding matters that may not be wrong but that are offensive to new and weak LCU members (1 Cor. 8:1–13 BP).
- A pattern of misuse of their special "love meals" together, so that some get food and others are left out (1 Cor. 11:17–34 BP).
- One-upmanship about whom can be more spectacularly "spiritual" in using the so-called "spiritual gifts." Again there is an utter lack of concern (1 Cor. 12–14 BP).
- Waffling on, or even outright denial of, central teachings (1 Cor. 15:12 BP).
- Unenthusiastic sharing of financial resources needed by the body (1 Cor. 16:2 BP).

I am struck by the fact that each of these characteristics has popped up at Glencrest and most other competition franchises, even without much effort on my part. It seems that humans are so prone toward these turpitudes that they might fall to them even without our help. I would agree that these tendencies seem to have progressed to satisfying conclusions in the Corinthian business unit.

Hotspur Memorandum Four

To: flambeau@darkcorp.com
From: hotspur@darkcorp.com
Subject: Schemes, plots, and designs

It's good to see that you have finally begun to comply with your assigned project.

Before we get to that, let me soften the exultant tone of my communication in memorandum one. Snarfless, a colleague who accidentally hacked into my correspondence files, reminded me via a critical memo to my section chief that I should not be so cocky while so many LCUs remain Competition franchises.

You may have heard about Snarfless's unfortunate accident. Whatever was the poor demon doing so close to the edge of the bottomless pit?

But back to the matter at hand.

Some LCUs are quite annoying. Nor, despite all of our intelligence, can we decipher precisely how the CEO's son's visit to humanity raised such authority and confidence among them. I read their reasoning, and I understand it no more clearly than I did before.

I read in your memo that you believe my advice is "insightful." If there is a note of anything except honor in your "admiration," we will let it pass, for now. Save sarcasm for your clients.

I am more gratified that you realize a carefully guarded secret: Much of what passes for our success is not the result of any great tempting skill. These human toads always seem to jump in the right directions whenever we goose them. Remember that your Gene and his LCU are ripe for the plucking if you use the tools provided by pioneering demons at places like Corinth.

Back in the Competition's Business Plan (2 Cor. 2:11), Paul warned his Corinthian clientele of our strategies. He called them "schemes" or "devices." The word he used can refer to plots or wiles.

Works for me.

So what's a wile? The most satisfying is one in which a client thinks she's getting the hang of this "goodness" trip. Then you do something that blows the lid off of her natural selfish depravity. This is called lack of integrity or hypocrisy. It works best in individual clients, but it can wash a lot of other spiders down the wall to their defeat.

Here's an example—it's an old wile to be sure, but it can't be surpassed. The client of one of my colleagues worked in one of the human education establishments as a football coach. Humans take these amusements quite seriously, so they can be quite useful diversions. Buck was one of the best at the tactics of the sport. He could take an unexceptional group of college athletes and leave another team in the dust by taking advantage of the opposition's weaknesses.

Because of Buck's extraordinary success with his college team, they made a spectacular finish in rankings one year. Top college and even professional programs were lining up at Buck's door, with their bucks in hand.

"Don't worry," he told his assistants. He was committed to his school, committed to the players.

"I'm here for the long haul," he assured players and potential recruits.

"Prepare my contract extension," he advised concerned school administrators.

"I'm not going anywhere," he replied to the reporters when they asked him about his meetings with agents for other teams.

As one newspaper sports columnist later put it, Buck "pulled off the liar's triple crown: First, he lied to his athletic director. Second, he lied to his assistants by mapping out a week's recruiting itinerary the day before he resigned to take a lucrative position elsewhere. Third, he lied to high school recruits and their parents who wanted to come to the school if he would be coach. His assigned tempter wept tears of joy.

That, Flambeau, is the kind of deceit-based strategy that our Debased Leader is looking for. There should be a special award for someone who can look a high school senior in the eye and say, "I'll be here until I retire," and to another, "We're going to win a lot of games together," then bail out less than twenty-four hours later. You've got to love it.

You can pull off the same sort of coup in your assigned LCU. It will surprise and hurt them a lot more than it did in the world of football. The Competition's folk are expected to behave with honesty. After all, they are "holy."

Regarding your musings and speculations, I guess this is the best I can expect from you, given all the influence you received from Scraptus. He was a one-track demon, not a scholar in any sense.

I hope you noticed in setting out the weaknesses of the Corinthians that strong relationships run throughout the list. The second and third open the door to all the others. First, human beings have been designed with a desire for wisdom. The Competition's Founder wired them that way because He wanted them to look to Him for truth. What a joke on Him when our CEO Below turned that desire to His advantage. The key word in your statement is *sophisticated*. You simply must keep their minds focused on the latest fad thinking. They automatically will take that thinking into the LCU when they gather. And the virus spreads through the system.

And as their thinking is turned toward the "truths" that we set before our clients, their lives drift naturally into that pervasive carnality you mentioned. They shut out the words of their CEO. Now put them together and you can infect the whole crew with our agenda for thinking and our agenda for living.

But get on with the assignment, Flambeau. As you continue reading 2 Corinthians, I want you to consider the context and setting of each reference to our Debased Leader. Some of these references are obvious, others will appear somewhat cryptic. Once you find them, check what the Competition's top management team understands about our strategic approach.

Once you learn what they know about our actions, you can see what the Competition wants to do to frustrate us. That will help you counter their actions. Needless to say, we intend to hinder every one of our clients from playing a successful part in their schemes.

I want a detailed series of strategic initiatives that will enable you to successfully secure the services of Gene and other potential clients from the Competition's local franchise at Glencrest once and for all. We will move beyond Scraptus's dilly-dallying and your feeble attempts. These pitiful creatures simply must serve our Pernicious Founder. Takeover is essential! Otherwise you'll feel the heat of my hot spur where you'll wish you hadn't.

For all of his failings, I should say that Scraptus did a fairly accurate job of communicating the abilities that are available from our Debased Excellence. I don't intend for you to abandon the decent tactics Scraptus taught. Low Command agrees that these cleverly crafted abilities, or "gifts" as he labeled them, can be used to take over the Competition's assets.

However, we must diversify your effort, and add to your arsenal of tools and resources.

Strategic Initiative One:
Cultivating Conflict

I determined this within myself, that I would not come again to you in sorrow. For if I make you sorrowful, then who is he who makes me glad but the one who is made sorrowful by me?

And I wrote this very thing to you, lest, when I came, I should have sorrow over those from whom I ought to have joy, having confidence in you all that my joy is the joy of you all. For out of much affliction and anguish of heart I wrote to you, with many tears, not that you should be grieved, but that you might know the love which I have so abundantly for you.

But if anyone has caused grief, he has not grieved me, but all of you to some extent—not to be too severe. This punishment which was inflicted by the majority is sufficient for such a man, so that, on the contrary, you ought rather to forgive and comfort him, lest perhaps such a one be swallowed up with too much sorrow. Therefore I urge you to reaffirm your love to him. For to this end I also wrote, that I might put you to the test, whether you are obedient in all things. Now whom you forgive anything, I also forgive. For if indeed I have forgiven anything, I have forgiven that one for your sakes in the presence of Christ, lest Satan should take advantage of us; for we are not ignorant of his devices. (2 Cor. 2:1–11 BP)

Flambeau Memorandum Two

To: hotspur@darkcorp.com
From: flambeau@darkcorp.com
Subject: Strategic Initiative 1: Cultivating Conflict

As I worked my way through Paul's somewhat rambling communiqué of 2 Corinthians in the Competition's Business Plan, I discovered six references to the Top Guy Below. In each, the Competition's vice president points out a particular "satanic strategy." I hate to mention it, but he seems to be plugged into us somewhere.

Here are our principles that Paul digs up:

1. Plant and cultivate seeds of conflict through harsh unforgiveness at their local competition units.
2. Mind-blind those whose corporate allegiance belongs to us, in order to prevent the Competition from really recruiting them.
3. Link individuals, and entire units if possible, to joint ventures that involve them in our own interests.
4. Promote false beliefs and confusion about the progress of our spiritual war with them and their CEO and His Son.
5. In a related maneuver, make teachings of Our Debased Leader sound like their Founder's own "enlightened truth."
6. Intimidate and discourage the Competition with painful life experiences.

I believe these six are all strategic initiatives from our corporate objectives. Let me begin by expanding on initiative one, "planting and cultivating seeds of conflict," which I believe is implied by 2 Corinthians 2:1–11 in their BP.

I learned from the first communiqué to this LCU that one of our clients became sexually involved with his stepmother (1 Cor. 5 BP). It was a tasty, sordid development. I know that sexual misadventure is a fairly simple temptation. What seems subtler is the way our operatives kept insisting that there was no problem with this liaison.

Who would have expected them to use that audacious argument? They did it by exhorting the LCU to treat this couple with the sort of acceptance and love they would never find outside the LCU. They should be more broadminded in their approach. There was no reason to condemn a person who was involved in a loving and mutually uplifting relationship. And if they did not accept the man and woman, the LCU would lose them. In fact, they made noises very much like Paul's argument in the first reference to our Infernal Leader in 2 Corinthians 2:1–11. The only difference was that they didn't want the LCU to bother with the negative aspects of punishment and exhorting repentance.

Paul demanded that forgiveness and restoration had to come after the offense was confessed and dealt with. Before repentance could occur, we were able to split the LCU through our "broadmindedness" initiative. After repentance, we shifted strategy to attempt to split the LCU through our "hang 'em high" initiative. Either way, the value we sought to produce was division through the LCU's handling of offenses. The vice president seems well aware of this from his words in 2 Corinthians 2:10–11:

> Now whom you forgive anything, I also forgive. For if indeed I have forgiven anything, I have forgiven that one for your sakes in the presence of Christ, lest Satan should take advantage of us; for we are not ignorant of his devices.

Until the vice president blew his stack in his first letter, the broadmindedness advocates managed to pull off a double-coup on our behalf. They introduced an excuse for moral defilement and at the same time made their response of "love" into a new controversy to divide the LCU.

I'm sure such agents were suitably honored when the time came for them to join us.

Then after Paul's first instruction, other spokespersons for division were empowered to voice self-righteous indignation over the possibility that this damaged sexual pervert might ever be considered for readmission.

Hotspur, when we are able to play both sides like that, our criteria for victory become a little confusing for me to follow. If someone from the other side is plugged in to us, it must drive them crazy.

Paul stifled our first initiative effectively when he called on the LCU to surrender this human to our CEO Below so that we could destroy him (1 Cor. 5:4–5 BP). I assume that is a good thing, though the ideal would have been for the man and his loving step-mother to sit publicly holding hands with each other through every service. It looks as if the woman was not a part of the assembly, since only the man was mentioned. On the surface, his discipline does not look like a very good development for us.

Disciplining LCU offenders happens so rarely, but when there is discipline I assume that means we've been successful. But it also means we've been caught being successful. And with each discipline there's always the chance for "repenting," which cannot be a good thing.

Assuming the man referred to in the second communication is the same as the one Paul condemns in 1 Corinthians, the Corinth LCU evidently came down pretty hard on him. That must have caused some serious trauma in the LCU. But the man seems to have repented, which is not a good thing. Paul told the people to take him back as one of them. If he had really changed to the worse, that would have meant an ultimate defeat for our side, wouldn't it?

On the other hand, won't he always be remembered for what he did in the LCU, and won't people outside the LCU misunderstand if they make up with such a notorious person?

Whatever else happened, I suppose the main point is that dissention erupted both times, which is even better in some ways than someone's sexual misconduct.

I conclude from this that we can pull victory out of failure if we can cause divisive parties to organize and beat the war drums. This is a strategy worth trying on Gene. I've tried planting complaints about the unit managers in his mind. I'll do more of this if you think it wise.

In regard to planting controversy, I see that almost any story can work. The people had accused Paul of changing his mind about coming to them. They were like children who said he didn't care for them (1 Cor. 1:15–24 BP).

Reading between the lines, it would seem that he cared a lot more for them than they did for him. They inflicted a lot of pain on him, and from our vantage point, pain inflicted on competition leaders has to be good. That is one thing I learned from Scraptus that surely must be true. People suffering frustration and pain give little attention to figuring out what we are trying to achieve.

Hotspur Memorandum Five

To: flambeau@darkcorp.com
From: hotspur@darkcorp.com
Subject: Moral messes and trivialities

I'm mildly surprised and pleased that you discovered all six references to Our Infernal Founder. I suppose I was more surprised that the Competition's vice-president could identify them in such detail.

That disclosure has been less damaging than you might suspect. You identified strategies that we developed in places like Corinth. They have been used to guide our efforts with Local competition units ever since. And the little fools are so stupid that they still fall for them more often than not.

Of course things have gotten easier in recent years, now that most of the LCUs have taken to discounting most of what Paul said as "culturally conditioned" to apply only to first-century Greek society. But even those who do believe these letters are true in theory can be prevented from studying and practicing them. When they talk about these letters, we can frequently get them stuck on superficialities. And even when they "get it" and get a good view of what Paul is saying to them and their LCU, they perversely run off and do the very things that they have been warned about.

Sometimes the livestock can be surprisingly resistant to being driven, because the Competition has somehow managed to put His presence inside them. But put them in a herd, and any neophyte tempter can spook them into a stampede. Cultivating conflict means spooking them in two directions at once, so that they stampede point blank into one another. It is notoriously easy to do. What can the Competition be thinking with this sort of organization? That's His problem. Ours is to make the most of these flaws in the lives of Gene and other clients.

Now for some specific advice in response to your analysis of strategic initiative number one.

I'm sure you are aware that the best policy is to do everything you can to keep your clients and the LCUs mired in moral messes on the one hand and trivialities on the other. These are the ideal responses to that sophisticated thinking and carnality mentioned above. Remember—carnality is the key to confusion, and confusion breaths destruction into conflict.

Of course the link between the flagrant immorality in their first Corinthian memo and the conflict that was tearing at the body is obvious. Corinth was a marketing sample in which we tested this approach. As you know from your Historic Temptation classes, the Corinthian LCU never did resolve their conflicts and split about twenty years after Paul was transferred to corporate headquarters. Yes, Corinth proved the effectiveness of making moral pratfalls a key component of our business plan.

Hieracles, a colleague of mine, succeeded in involving his client at Corinth sexually with his stepmother. That was a particularly brilliant move, because Corinth was such a jaded city. It was difficult to do something sexually innovative enough to be shocking. However, even the city libertines drew the line at the sort of behavior that some in the LCU were justifying. When the local management team tried to step in, a number of our clients insisted that condemnation was judgmental and unloving. Condemnation only kept this loving couple from having a full relationship with the other members of the LCU and with the CEO Himself. Worse, look what it would do to recruiting others into the LCU. Those with similarly creative interpersonal relationships would not feel accepted.

And enough members bought this line that the managers were

stifled. No one thought that Hieracles and his team could pull off such a ploy, but we have been using their maneuver successfully ever since.

Of course, when he heard of it, the Competition's vice president, Paul, saw through the ploy and went into apoplexy. He actually called on them to surrender the client to our CEO Below so we could destroy him (1 Cor. 5:4–5 BP). We intended to do that soon enough anyway. The woman had long been a loyal operative for us. She was the bait to catch this little mouse, and the mouse snared an entire LCU.

Flambeau Memorandum Three

To: hotspur@darkcorp.com
From: flambeau@darkcorp.com
Subject: So get to the point already!

I have heard all of these old war stories for centuries now. So far as I can tell from the record, the Hieracles Maneuver was not nearly so successful as some of you supervisors like to boast. Didn't their vice president come up with a gambit to shut down the sexual immorality? Though it seems they were hard on the fellow.

How about some strategies that are guaranteed to work?

Hotspur Memorandum Six

To: flambeau@darkcorp.com
From: hotspur@darkcorp.com
Subject: The "point" is broadminded intolerance

Guarantees? You just don't get it, do you? Their CEO always has a countermeasure—*always*. You have to work the situation to milk all the damnation out of a maneuver that you can, while you can.

Actually, it is easier to use what you call "immorality" as a tactic now than it was at the start. Your clients aren't accustomed to anyone telling them that what they want to do is wrong. Dare they use the "S" word? Accusing someone of "sin" is to invite them to be highly offended. They can be counted on to spread gossip about the leaders. They can always go to a more enlightened LCU down the road. They can even sue for the defamation of their good name.

The Hieracles Maneuver was as successful as anything could be against their vice president Paul. He was one of our most vexing opponents. When Paul stepped in with his letter, we did eventually run into trouble, but we had done considerable damage to that LCU by then, and a number of clients had left in disgust. That letter from Paul stirred the managers to begin the discipline countermaneuver.

You seem to have the usual one-dimensional forensic understanding of discipline, Flambeau. Someone does wrong and gets hauled to the tar and feathers. It's fine that they think that, but you should know better. The discipline process can help us so long as they identify it only with the Salem witch trials. LCU discipline that is only seen as negative is always divisive. If they somehow get the idea that it is intended to build, nurture, restore, and unite the people, we are in trouble. From their CEO's viewpoint, the idea of discipline is that of mature people gently guiding their weaker brothers and sisters toward maturity. *Discipline* describes the whole process that they call discipleship.

So everything you are doing is supposed to be keeping discipline's teaching and nurture from happening. If it isn't happening, and you can engineer some failure in Gene's life, for example, then any attempt on the Competition's part to bring him back into line will seem arbitrary and unjust. You might even convince Gene that his rights have been violated so egregiously that he'll file a legal action in the secular courts. We've pulled that off a number of times in recent decades.

You may note from the lengthy time required to bring one of their little squawlers to adulthood that humans require a lot of maturing. And maturing means continually realizing they have not yet arrived, accepting this humility, and submitting to someone else's authority. Your task is to equate "humility" with "humiliation." How these little worms despise being humiliated. Fear of humiliation can make them resent every appearance of authority. Of course their Business Plan makes it clear that none of them stops being a disciple until they die. So even the leaders who disciple are to be submissive disciples themselves. These leaders can have the largest heads of all, so they often squeal the loudest about being molded. If you can make the managers self-righteously offended at what the client has done, you can stir up no end of trouble for the LCU, and the offender and managers all will walk away crushed in spirit. Scraptus taught you something about the power of discouragement, didn't he?

If discipline poses a problem in cultivating confusion and dissention, ego poking is the solution. You noticed that you don't see much discipline going on today. Our agents have worked hard to guard against it—especially the constructive day-to-day maturing sort. Without that, we'll be glad to encourage the other if they aren't too cowardly to try it. Then if our individual successes are noticed in the LCU, we can let our clients twist in the wind and attack the entire group.

Regarding your question about forgiveness, even embryonic-level demons such as yourself should know there is no tolerance for this. As you noted, our agents were able to reverse the attitudes of their clients from tolerant acceptance of the man's affair with his stepmother to harsh criticism after his "change of mind." They came down so hard on the guy they nearly succeeded in crushing his spirit.

That's why Paul called on them to "back off" on the punishment they had inflicted and forgive (2 Cor. 2:6, 7 BP).

Encourage false tolerance all you can, Flambeau, but *never ever allow genuine forgiveness.* Clients must always be prevented from extending such weak, sentimental tripe. You read their vice president's words in 2 Corinthians 2:7: "You ought to forgive and comfort him." If that's their aim, ours is the opposite. Remember—zero forgiveness equals zero encouragement and unlimited potential for conflict.

Allow a client to forgive, and I can just about guarantee that you'll be facing a quick transfer to Siberia. I shouldn't have to remind you that an attitude of superiority and intolerance is the best antidote to this forgiveness rubbish. Go back and study the early Pharisees in the Competition's BP. Theirs is the attitude I want to see at Glencrest.

One thing to watch for in the more serious negative discipline is the fact that their CEO's Son gave them a working judicial process to follow in Matthew 18 of their BP. This method of dealing with offending brothers and sisters is designed to neutralize our operations at both the individual and corporate ends. It can be quite damaging to our efforts if used by units that are carefully following the Competition's entire master plan. First, their discipline encourages the client to genuinely admit thoughts, attitudes, and actions that violate the CEO's wishes. If the offender does not, as they say, "repent," they exert increasing pressure. If nothing else works, they exclude the client from the LCU in order to erect a firewall between the virus and their operating system.

The humans of the generation you work with are of the mindset that they are something special in and of themselves. Their technological advances and lifestyle have made them, pound for pound, the largest, most easily bruised egos in human history. So they go miles out of their way to say and do the things they think are appropriate and will avoid hurting people's feelings. In the LCUs, if people are told that their lives are not in conformity to the Business Plan, they usually relocate to a more tolerant group down the street. If they think the LCU or its leaders have humiliated them publicly in negative discipline, some will not hesitate to retaliate, bringing the body into ruin through a lawsuit, "negative press," or gossip.

But don't let your guard down, just because things seem positive to our cause. They do occasionally counterattack from this point of weakness. Those who are genuinely in the Competition's employ still have the CEO's presence inside of them, and He has a habit of smashing their egos at just the point when it seems they are ruined for His use. If their egos are broken, they will be humiliated by what they have done more than by what people think of them. That is almost the worst of situations. The only thing that can be more damaging is if the others in the LCU accept the repentance, especially those who have been harmed personally by the offense.

Never, under any circumstance, allow one of your clients to go through the Competition's full treatment of discipline, brokenness, repentance, and restoration. Those people can be truly frightening.

Hotspur Memorandum Seven

To: flambeau@darkcorp.com
From: hotspur@darkcorp.com
Subject: Establishing moral tension

Although you recognize the importance of producing conflict, you must be careful not to underestimate the absolute usefulness of promoting moral tension. Realize that all humans have moral problems, and no one is more hypercritical than someone who has spotted in someone else a moral failing that he does not have.

No, that isn't altogether accurate. The most hypercritical person is someone who takes a mythical deduction on his income tax return, then jumps all over a shoplifter . . . or is addicted to on-line pornography but would stone an adulterer. We have an almost infinite variety of options when we play the moral tension game.

So that you can make use of this moral, or perhaps I should say immoral, tool more effectively, let me make some specific recommendations.

Pornography is a wonderful spur line to take because you can ease someone into it so gradually that he will never know he's in trouble. It can seem so innocent.

Surely you keep up with your study of demonotistics and know what a powerful tool we have in sexuality. It has never been more attractive to humans, especially the male of the species. Their Internet offers them about a million porn sites. I consider this one of our great recent achievements. One report from our cyberspace division insists that we have spilled sexual content over eighty percent of the World Wide Web.

With such a powerful human weakness and a readily available

source to sample with little fear of exposure, we have even been able to reach top LCU managers.

One of my own case files shows how effectively this works. Roger was a devoted husband, father of several young children, and actively involved in one of the Competition's LCUs. His job required him to spend several hours a week carrying out research online. Initially Roger shook his head in disgust when I steered his explorations to sites where unclothed members of the opposite sex brazenly invited him to sample the visual wares in total privacy.

Disgusted, maybe, but he was also intrigued. He had never been around that sort of thing to "spice up" his marriage. Before long he was spending more time on the porn sites than on company business. He purchased a state-of-the-art computer for home so the family could use educational resources and "stay connected" by e-mailing relatives. Imagine what happened when his wife discovered Roger's late-night connections. I gave him a double hit of a lost job and a lost family, and he still didn't give up his porn.

Your key target client, Gene, has not yet been exposed to a single pornography site. Flambeau, what have you been doing? If I were in your hooves, I'd find any excuse to get him onto the Web where he can "stumble" onto our delights. As you implement these strategic elements, I want you to continue your research. And if you don't get that client of yours on the Internet and have him sample the porn, you may find yourself sampling the same Siberian winters as your former mentor, Scraptus.

I assume that I should not have to say much about the standard sexual possibilities. Our cultural strategists have connected bits of sexual messages everywhere humans look with the beautiful notion that they should have freedom to do anything they like as long as it doesn't "hurt" anyone. It's part of that sophistication-plus-carnality factor I've told you about.

On television and in the movies, people are having a lot of fun with their "sexual expression." Male-female sexual experiences are even giving way to male-male and female-female sexual relationships. It has become simple to help your clients see the glamorous side of becoming sexually involved outside of marriage without considering bothersome consequences.

Jared, a client of mine, met his wife Connie at one of the Competition's primary training institutions. He was so respected that his picture and story were used for recruiting purposes. Jared and Connie started working together with teenagers. On a hunch, I encouraged a lonely divorcee named Lila to join Jared on an LCU team, on which they spent considerable time alone together in planning sessions. Once their physical attraction kicked in, it was a simple matter to arrange for her to need help starting her car and to flirt provocatively with Jared while he was helping her. His natural responses took care of the rest.

I made certain that it wasn't long before Connie suspected and discovered the affair. The marriage was shattered. Even better, Jared will have little credibility for serving the Competition again.

Flambeau Memorandum Four

To: hotspur@darkcorp.com
From: flambeau@darkcorp.com
Subject: What else should we be doing?

We have spent some time on our first initiative of cultivating conflict. I recognize that Paul here is mainly dealing with the issue of forgiving the repentant offender and closing ranks around him. I can't help thinking, however, that 2 Corinthians 2:11 has more in mind when Paul says they should be wary of our Pernicious Lordship's "devices."

I particularly wonder about the issue of ignorance. He doesn't want them to be "ignorant of his devices." I know that there's a reference to "mind-blinding" coming up later in the vice president's letter. Perhaps this reference to "devices" is used to alert readers to some of the ways that we sow discord and use both offenses and unforgiveness to blind the minds of those in the LCUs. We definitely don't want them to use judicial plans such as Matthew 18 correctly if we can help it. Nor do we want to have them reading the references to discipline in 1 Corinthians 5 and 2 Corinthians 2 in their Business Plan.

Is there something we can put into their water that keeps them ignorant of our devices? A magic stupidity bullet to shoot into their minds?

Hotspur Memorandum Eight

To: flambeau@darkcorp.com
From: hotspur@darkcorp.com
Subject: Circumventing the Competition's BP

I hope you were attempting to interject a (very) little humor in your last e-mail. You should know the answer to your question without thinking, or else Scraptus did an even worse job than I thought.

Certainly the "stupidity bullet" to breeding hostility, low integrity, and ineffectuality in any LCU is to keep clients from looking seriously at the Business Plan. It's easy to assume that they will not really be interested in the words of their CEO. Usually they are not. But some of them will fool you, just as Gene and his friends at Glencrest surprised you. Their study of the Plan has been at the root of your failure there. I just checked your progress. Gene and the others continue to look at the Business Plan obsessively. So maybe you are not aware of the continuing danger in this.

I know the excuse: It is difficult to keep some of the more committed groups out of the Plan when that is the main reason they are coming together. True, so what do you suppose we do about it? Even you should know the answer to this question— you give them some other main reasons for meeting. Then the Plan won't get in the way of causing conflict.

Here's a tip for determining what sort of distractions to employ: Eavesdrop on the ten minutes before their meetings. There are two general categories of LCUs. At one sort, the people know each other and enjoy being together. They can do a lot of visiting before things get started. Some may raise their voices to be heard over the music when it starts. They secretly wish the musicians would keep down the racket.

These LCUs are built around fellowship.

At the other sort of meetings, all is reverent and quiet until the first notes of the organ and choir break the stillness. These LCUs speak in hushed whispers, if at all, as they wait for things to get started. Occasionally a soft snore can be heard. These units are built around reverence and vertical worship. They may not know one another well. Their attitude is strictly "down-to-business."

It might seem that we should prefer the first sort. Sometimes. However, these fellowshippers are notoriously adept at switching mental gears to do some serious meeting with the CEO, while the more reverent types may be just about feeling without any substance. The fellowship-oriented body can meet together for Plan study and spend all but ten minutes happily munching finger foods and sharing "prayer requests" (i.e., gossiping). They can continually be distracted from the Business Plan unless some spoilsport squawks about their lack of discipline and pulls them back to the task.

The second group can be kept easily from the CEO's plan by uplifting poetic but nonsensical or kindergarten-level meditations. Dramatic and musical extravaganzas can keep them out of the Business Plan for weeks on end. These people usually have rather decided opinions about what is good music for the meeting and what is not. They will entertain you for months with bitter conflict on the subject, forgetting the larger point of why they meet.

At one time, this problem of Business Plan study was more serious than it has been of late. We have secured a great many of their LCU management training centers. The right managers will see to it that no one takes the Business Plan seriously. Just know for now that your job is to make sure they stay focused on the superficialities and live under a veneer of appropriateness. Then they won't be at risk of digging in and learning what holiness really is and how we counter it. Meanwhile, keep your own mind focused on what we don't want them to know—our Infernal Master's plan. I intend to see to it that you get a firm grip on that big picture, whatever it takes.

Vice president Paul had a dangerous level of comprehension of our takeover strategies. Remember that he was one of our corporate agents before he sold out. That's why you must study what he has to say.

Hotspur Memorandum Nine

To: flambeau@darkcorp.com
From: hotspur@darkcorp.com
Subject: Swinging the pendulum

Inexperienced tempters often run across clients who are resistant to enticement. They just refuse to be dragged into moral messes. On rare occasions, even I find an obstinate client. That's when the Corinth example becomes an important aid.

If you can't tempt them into the obvious, showy sins, get them going the other direction into pride and self-satisfaction. Those without a talent for the obvious sins are quick to stone those who are good at them. Pharisaism is the ultimate sucker punch. Those committed to the Competition are prone to the most delicious forms of self-righteousness. And moral pagans are the best of all. They are almost unrecruitable by the Competition since they think they have already arrived at sufficient goodness. They are so surprised when they die and suddenly find themselves with us. They're just sure that there's been a paperwork error somewhere up the line. There are those who have been here since the CEO's Son was on earth, and they are still waiting for their transfer orders.

When someone is caught in what the Competition labels "flagrant sin," generally one of two responses will occur. Some, as we noted earlier, will be incensed and try to get the local competition unit to punish the individual harshly. Others will be broadminded and call for tolerance and forgiveness. Either extreme works well for our purposes. Simply determine in which direction each client is leaning, then push—hard—away from a balanced perspective. There are always enough vocal people to stir up plenty of conflict.

You may be tired of my repeating this analysis, Flambeau, but if you would just once get it right I wouldn't have to keep harping on it. Personally, I prefer to push my own clients toward righteous indignation. That gives them the appearance of conforming to the Competition's agenda, while actually serving their own. Never forget the example of our Pharisee clients who were about to stone an adulterous woman. They were expressing proper outrage toward this wretch, while protecting the man with whom she had been caught. They seemed to have an opportunity to trap the CEO's Son into joining the lynch mob. He certainly should have been indignant.

Nothing worked with Him.

This entire strategy of pushing toward indignation or overtolerance is called "swinging the pendulum." Corinth is a classic example of its use. From being too accepting and forgiving, the people became overly harsh.

I was assigned to look after a man named Wilson, who thought he should be part of the leadership team. He was extremely familiar with their Business Plan and could quote it endlessly at meetings. He was a great conflict starter. What no one knew was that he was not only overly critical but also could lose his temper at home. He hit his wife one night, and it felt good. Things reached the point when his wife's clothing almost always covered bruises from his blows.

Rumors spread and finally were confirmed. Some were certain that this should be dealt with through a strong discipline process. But we persuaded them of the advantages of taking a tolerant approach, and anger management counseling was recommended. Since going to a counselor admitted weakness, though, my macho client got out of that quickly enough.

One day his wife showed up at the LCU sporting a black eye. She filed for legal separation. Then my colleagues and I persuaded the same clients who had tried to excuse the husband to take a strong stand against marital separation. They actually had her thrown out of the choir. That, Flambeau, is how the pendulum works.

Strategic Initiative Two: Mind-blinding

Now the Lord is the Spirit; and where the Spirit of the Lord is, there is liberty. But we all, with unveiled face, beholding as in a mirror the glory of the Lord, are being transformed into the same image from glory to glory, just as by the Spirit of the Lord.

Therefore, since we have this ministry, as we have received mercy, we do not lose heart.

But we have renounced the hidden things of shame, not walking in craftiness nor handling the word of God deceitfully, but by manifestation of the truth commending ourselves to every man's conscience in the sight of God. But even if our gospel is veiled, it is veiled to those who are perishing, whose minds the god of this age has blinded, who do not believe, lest the light of the gospel of the glory of Christ, who is the image of God, should shine on them.

For we do not preach ourselves, but Christ Jesus the Lord, and ourselves your bondservants for Jesus' sake. For it is the God who commanded light to shine out of darkness who has shone in our hearts to give the light of the knowledge of the glory of God in the face of Jesus Christ. (2 Cor. 3:17–4:6 BP)

Flambeau Memorandum Five

To: hotspur@darkcorp.com
From: flambeau@darkcorp.com
Subject: Tying on the blindfold

Mind-blinding means distorting the mental processes of clients still unaffiliated with the Competition so that they won't be able to respond to recruitment. When I read the 2 Corinthians portion of their Business Plan, I gained a greater appreciation for the fact that these human clients really belong to us. Some initiative must be taken by the Competition if they are to change allegiance from our corporate message. I am aware, however, of the many appeals by their management team to engage in active recruiting. These efforts come up under a variety of archaic sounding headings: evangelism, discipleship, outreach, missions. . . .

The proliferation of these efforts, in my opinion, bolsters the position that human assets default to us unless recruited and acquired. For example, their CEO, in His final motivational address before returning to the home office, urged them to, "Go and make disciples of all nations" (Matt. 28:19 BP). Such a strategic appeal would be unnecessary unless their CEO assumed that we would hold the human assets unless the Competition takes them away from us. Paul urged the young entrepreneur he mentored, Timothy, to learn the principles of the Business Plan and commit these to a succession of humans who would then pass them on to others (2 Tim. 2:2 BP). Clearly their top management has felt it necessary from the beginning to exert heroic efforts in numerous recruiting campaigns.

Based on this observation, it seems that our job should be easier than I at first thought it might be. After all, if they have a natural tendency to gravitate to the darkness, like their cockroaches, we should find it fairly easy to keep them away from the light.

Another thing I find intriguing is that their vice president, Paul, would give so much credit to our CEO Below. Referring to him as "the god of this age" seems to give him—and by extension his corporate objectives—quite a bit of credence. Is this still consistent with their attitude toward the Top Guy Down Below? If so, can we prompt them to give our Debased Leader some of the kudos and credit they think belongs to their CEO? After all, he once occupied an important place in their hierarchy, since their Business Plan refers to him as the "Anointed Cherub" in Ezekiel 28:14. It would be easy for us to point out that role. I shall look to you for direction as to how to best take advantage of whatever credit they give him. This would seem to increase their curiosity about him and accord him the accolades he deserves.

Hotspur Memorandum Ten

To: flambeau@darkcorp.com
From: hotspur@darkcorp.com
Subject: Mind-blinding and His Low Majesty

You raise the issue of seeking to elevate the status of our Debased Eminence among humans. That's an interesting point, one on which our top strategists differ. Historically we have taken the position that it's more profitable for the spotlight to be turned away from our efforts. The CEO Below gets his honor after we have brought our clients safely through their time on earth. His Lowness also takes pleasure when objects are dedicated to his honor. A few groups have given homage to him directly by name, thinking that with him on their side they could have all their desires.

Poor slobs, they've never caught on to the fact that we need not give them anything. Why bait the hook when the fish are eager to jump into the net?

Our more progressive planners, however, share your desire that we take a higher profile, and recently we've been attempting some things that seem somewhat effective.

Honor for honor's sake is worthless to our cause, but with honor comes the power to intimidate. In many places, their Business Plan refers to our boss as "Satan," which, as you know, means "adversary." You can look these up in their Business Plan in Job 1:6; Matthew 4:10; Acts 5:3; and Revelation 12:9.

We aren't particularly helped when they know that we are close by. That can simply make them more skittish and wary. But if we can build the fear factor, all they think about are bad consequences. We both know that we are restricted in what we can do to them.

They become obsessed with "spiritual warfare" and begin to see our CEO as a near equal with theirs.

That's where the tactic of ascribing the work of their CEO to ours can be fruitful.

Never discount our leader as the ultimate intimidator, Flambeau. The Competition's very first VP of operations, Peter, referred to our CEO as a "roaring lion" in his part of the Business Plan (1 Peter 5:8). He was warning their people to be disciplined so they could avoid falling to our strong temptations. We don't want information about that getting out.

But suppose people recall just the "roaring lion" part, remembering about how it's "a jungle out there" in their daily world of work? Suddenly they think they see us on every street corner. They know how effectively we place ideas of violence into our clients. Most recently we've raised the pressure level of frustration and stress to the red zone in some clients, then aimed them out onto the highways, schools, and sports centers to vent their rage. We've recruited and trained them to carry out acts so violent that they surprise even me, from blowing up hotel crowds and buses to crashing airliners into buildings.

All of that serves to keep the world disrupted, but don't forget the important side benefit of keeping the clients in our opposition's camp fearful. Fearful people are blinded so that they forget what they have going for them. They don't get excited about evangelism. Then they would be bringing more problems into their nice safe LCUs. They start looking at people with olive skin as potential terrorists instead of potential brothers and sisters.

Flambeau Memorandum Six

To: hotspur@darkcorp.com
From: flambeau@darkcorp.com
Subject: Mind-blinding and light

In studying the initiative of mind-blinding in this portion of the Competition's Business Plan, I may have discovered one of the reasons my client Gene chose to connect with them and dropped his affiliation with us. Paul spoke here of their corporate message as "the light of the gospel of the glory of Christ." Then he went on to say, "We do not preach ourselves, but Christ Jesus the Lord" (2 Cor. 4:4–5 BP).

I've already noticed how hard it is to counter a message that focuses on the person of their CEO's Son. At Corinth, it seems we were somewhat successful in deflecting that focus. I understand that Paul here is not talking about our work at Corinth precisely. He seems to be referring to what we did in the Jewish hearts to blind them to the gospel of their Messiah. However, permitting into the LCU a number of those for whom the gospel was veiled by their traditions only added to the factions by which we sowed division. As mentioned before, there were "factions" in the LCU who even ranked their favorite leader ahead of their CEO's Son (1 Cor. 1:12 BP).

All sorts of veiling were taking place to obscure the message of our Competition. The Jewish veiling was the most notable and the most successful. As the message was veiled, mind-blinded agents of ours placed their own interests out front and called for others to back them.

I'm convinced that it was the focus on a person rather than an agenda or business paradigm that brought about the change in the life of my client. The strength of that focus caught me off guard, I'll admit. I intend to be more careful with my clients who have not yet responded to the Competition's corporate line.

Paul says that when one turns to the Competition, veils are pulled back so one can see. It sounds as if there's a point beyond which there isn't a lot we can do in blinding the minds of individual clients.

Hotspur Memorandum Eleven

To: flambeau@darkcorp.com
From: hotspur@darkcorp.com
Subject: Blinding the Competition's clients

Occasionally I see glimmers of potential in you, Flambeau.

Yes, there is a point beyond which we are powerless to keep our clients from switching allegiance to the Competition. However, that problem usually occurs because we failed to do our job adequately. I consider this one of your prime weaknesses, and a flaw in the work carried out by many of your contemporaries. It's a shortcoming that will surely cost you if clients get too close to the Competition's "light" or hear their message before we can corrupt it. Once they get reeled in that far, we should not feel surprised when they align themselves to the Competition for good.

Many of our clients follow the human sport of baseball. If the human who throws the ball aims it chest-high and chucks it fast, right in front of the one who wants to hit it, the "batter" is likely to blast the ball a long distance. That's precisely what the man throwing the ball, the "pitcher," does not want to happen.

Successful pitchers learn to keep the batter guessing about where the ball will go, never giving it to him where he can get a solid swipe at it.

Sometimes the Competition's top sales people become so focused on their message that they don't personally connect with their potential clients (who are still *our* clients). They just "dump the whole load" of their message and push for a response.

Briefly, they may succeed in pulling back the veil we have placed on the message, saying to the potential client, "Here, take a look at this. This is what you want." But any tempter worth his flames knows that a momentary distraction on our part can allow that veil to drop right back into place.

Suppose one of your clients wanders into one of their recruiting sessions and starts to become interested in the sales pitch. If that happens, all isn't lost. Just remind the individual that the meeting is dragging on far longer then it should, or that the speaker uses bad grammar or has a bit of a lisp. The room seems uncomfortably hot/cold, and isn't that Fred three rows up? Can't imagine why he's interested in things like this. And that was a funny story about the man and the insurance salesman. Didn't that same story go around before, only about a lawyer? Sure wish there had been time to catch a bite before the meeting. Man, those hunger pangs are getting intense. How much longer can this guy talk?

Keep this flow of distractions heading in, and the message will blow right on by.

I call my favorite tactic "putting it on the corners." Just as a pitcher confuses batters by putting a little spin on a "curveball," you can add a little "spin" to the Competition's message. That's exactly what was happening in their Business Plan when the minds of the people of Israel were confused. They wound up getting the idea that they could somehow keep the Business Plan rules and earn favor with the Competition. They kept bringing more sacrifices, instituting more religious activities. Finally, one of their early agents, a man named Isaiah, said the Founder was actually sickened by their efforts (Isa. 1:11–15 BP). We were ecstatic with that result!

You may not recall, Flambeau, that their whole corporate mission almost became sidetracked from the outset when we introduced agents into their very first franchise, the one in Jerusalem, to teach them that believers had to follow those old Jewish customs to be approved by their CEO (Acts 15:1 BP). That situation stirred up a delightful controversy (they called it "no small dispute") and a great deal of confusion. That confrontation is closely related to the problem of the message veiled to the Jews at Corinth. I rank that as one of our best jobs of putting a spin on the message.

This "doctrinal spin" can be used in a number of contemporary settings, including local competition units and training facilities.

Flambeau Memorandum Seven

To: hotspur@darkcorp.com
From: flambeau@darkcorp.com
Subject: Playing the spin

Finally we seem to be getting to some ideas that I can use to mind-blind. I've seen good results from this "spin game," but I'm not sure I understand exactly how it works.

The difficulty would seem to be the Business Plan. Most of the ways I can think to spin the truth involve teachings that are covered fairly thoroughly in the Business Plan. In the early times, during the days when the Business Plan was being written, it must have been easier to blind minds. But how does one go about it when all that the client has to do is pick up the Business Plan and straighten out the curveball?

I know you have said I must keep clients out of the BP, but isn't there more to it than that? It only takes a few who actually know the Plan to cause problems for all those who don't know it.

That appears to be one of the weaknesses with putting so much stock in what happened at Corinth. We today have to contend with the fact that our clients can be exposed to the Business Plan at a moment's notice. Keeping them away from meetings and quiet times only goes so far.

Maybe some examples of how it works would help.

Hotspur Memorandum Twelve

To: flambeau@darkcorp.com
From: hotspur@darkcorp.com
Subject: Throwing a curved message and messenger

Don't think that there's a shortcut substitute to your work of keeping clients out of the Business Plan. It's your single best strategy for blinding their minds. But there are tools that, when added to good basic diligence, will help. Let me give a couple of recent examples.

One of my colleagues, Floundus, was responsible for a local competition unit in the upper Midwest. His LCU was populated with people who supposedly had a strict interpretation of the Competition's Business Plan and a commitment to live it out.

After studying these tendencies carefully, Floundus introduced a couple into the LCU who were well versed in the Competition's corporate literature. But as a result of my colleague's influence over their studies, they had developed the notion that strict obedience to certain "legal" principles from the Business Plan is mandatory. This is spin, Flambeau. We take a good thing and make it a necessary, "you'll go to hell if you don't have it" thing.

This couple ridiculed the unqualified acceptance of one of the central tenets of the Competition's Business Plan—the part about "salvation" being a "free gift." In the broad picture it was true, they supposed, but in the nitty-gritty there were certain things one had to do to qualify for the free gift.

They used small group studies of the business literature to introduce their particular slant on the importance of demonstrating good works in a valid relationship with the Competition. The managers at this LCU did know the Business Plan, and they sought to confront this misuse of it. So Floundus prompted the couple to identify faults with the personal and family life and ministry of the lead manager. They poisoned the atmosphere until the manager was fired and other managers quit in disgust. That left the "purifying" leaders to bring in a compatible LCU leader. Before long this entire LCU had become a bastion for promoting one of our major corporate messages—that one must somehow add a set of personal good actions to what the CEO's Son did in order to qualify to join their company.

Carpless, a highly qualified demonic strategist, was placed in charge of one of the Competition's respected training units. You might consider this a difficult assignment, but he coordinated activities effectively with likely potential student and faculty demons. Ever so slowly he began to whisper the importance of achieving a more relevant, progressive, and academically balanced curriculum, while using gifted teachers who stood at the forefront of new theological initiatives.

Over several years, a number of free thinkers were hired to give balanced scholarship. These began to discuss "what is missing" to achieve scholarly renown and attract more donors. They called for curriculum reform, so that students would learn more about emotional power and less about content, more practical ministry management and less about interpretation of old words, more relevance and less naive parroting of dead orthodoxy.

Eventually these new reformers shifted emphasis toward the spectacular to draw in people. Miraculous experiences became necessary for participants in this training program to be considered valid members.

Imagine the stir—the conflict—when the national business unit investigated what was happening and demanded that these faculty be removed from their positions. In fact, a great many leaders had been through the altered program by then and took their ideas out into the LCUs. The school never returned to its previous stature, either in fact or in the minds of those in the national unit.

For his efforts, Carpless received a commendation from Low Command. Hopefully these two examples of ways to confound the message will generate some ideas and enable you to carry on some message diversion in the local franchise at Glencrest.

However, Flambeau, if you can't curve the message, at least put a little curve into the messenger. That seemed to be one of the major concerns expressed by the corporate brain trust of our Competition and their VP Paul. You surely recall his explanation that he and his colleagues had "renounced the hidden things of shame, not walking in craftiness nor handling the Word of God deceitfully" (2 Cor. 4:2 BP).

Perhaps that was true in his time, but I'm pleased to report that, in our day, many of the Competition's agents seem to delight in allowing hidden pockets of lust, greed, pride, and other virtues we extol to creep into both their personal lives and their message.

In many instances they've learned to pull the wool over the eyes of those to whom they communicate. The result—their agenda is thrown out of equilibrium when it is discovered that their walk doesn't match their message.

Flambeau Memorandum Eight

To: hotspur@darkcorp.com
From: flambeau@darkcorp.com
Subject: Mind-blinding and light

Your examples reminded me that I have not yet made an in-depth study of the role that professional staff members—LCU heads—play in our mind-blinding games with clients such as Gene. Clearly their VP, Paul, can serve as a prototype for middle management leaders at contemporary local competition units.

These people sometimes see right through the pitches you have mentioned. So maybe what we need to do is put a spin on their ministry. In the early days after the CEO's Son organized this model of LCU there seems to have been a more bottom-up organization, in which each person owned enough stock to provide a clear self-identification with the ministry. Now the people act more like consumers for whom ministry is done, top down. I suspect that must leave them extremely vulnerable to viruses we may introduce through the leaders.

It strikes me that these middle management types provide one of the keys to gaining an increased influence over clients like Gene. They are, after all, charged with spreading the "light" of the Competition's message, and Paul seems most solicitous in this portion of the Business Plan (2 Cor. 4:1) that leaders such as himself would not lose heart.

There was a great deal at Corinth to make anyone from the Competition lose heart, but now that I think of it, there are plenty of things at Glencrest that would make most people give up. If the leaders lose heart, I assume they must lose perspective, spending less time anchoring themselves in the Business Plan as they expend all of their energies on personal, family, and corporate crises. That seems a solid form of mind-blinding. Perhaps I should consider introducing the middle manager here at the Glencrest local franchise to some of the more intimidating aspects of our corporate culture.

Then, of course, Paul in the next verse (4:2) gets to the other aspect of losing heart, the one with which I am more familiar. I prefer these straightforward temptations of sex, money, ego, and bitterness that Paul says he has renounced. These "hidden things" are always good for shame and guilt. Plus, as it says here, they help adulterate the message.

Are we overdoing the subtlety bit, Hotspur? What if I concentrate on disheartening these modern "Pauls" and adulterating their light?

Hotspur Memorandum Thirteen

To: flambeau@darkcorp.com
From: hotspur@darkcorp.com
Subject: Diffusing the light

There is some validity in what you say about working the LCU from the top down. If you had been paying attention, you would have noticed that a lot of my instruction already assumes this.

But remember, Flambeau, we cannot do just anything we please to their employees, even at the management level. Their CEO has guaranteed that He will only let us go so far, and they will have sufficient resources against us (1 Cor. 10:13; 2 Peter 1:3–4 BP). The old saying still holds true: "Don't put all of your temptations into one fireball." When it comes to effective tempting, diversity is crucial.

When we try to blind the minds of those who are committed to the opposition CEO, that presence He has placed in their pathetic little hearts has the power to stop us cold. So, to answer your question about being too subtle, subtlety in infiltrating the LCU or solidifying our hold on dabblers in their operations can be far more practical than attempting to directly delude or permanently twist the minds of genuinely committed Competition workers.

With that caveat, there are some things we can do to filter the light nicely for our purposes, even if we cannot block it out completely. Some people are beyond blinding, but they can be turned quite myopic.

Some time ago, Low Command assigned a new member of our executive staff, Drachus, to blunt the growing influence of an international media unit.

We'd had success twenty years before in this organization.

Another of our tempters instigated a sexual liaison between one of the organization's most visible executives and a coworker. This man left his wife to marry the woman and had to be removed by this agency. He in turn filed a lawsuit, which led to an incredible amount of adverse publicity. We thought it would sink them for good. However, after a time, this agency was able to secure the services of a good leader and move beyond the incident.

After studying the history of this division of the Competition's communication mechanism, Drachus decided it was time to launch a similar initiative. I won't bother you with the details, Flambeau, but what he did was outstanding. He arranged for a series of encounters between this new executive and an attractive woman with whom he came in contact.

The man had developed a high resistance to any kind of sexual impropriety, especially given the story of his predecessor. However, Drachus worked overtime to lower the perception of this man that there was anything wrong with the increasing amount of time he was spending with this woman. Then Drachus brought the intense emotional relationship to the attention of others with whom the man worked.

The result was absolutely combustible. Though the man and woman had not committed adultery, the man wound up resigning in shame. Many who had been positively influenced accepted the suggestion that "you can't trust anything those people say. They just don't back it up with their lives."

Variations on this strategy are being played out every day among local competition units. The most effective course of action usually involves connecting those high-minded professional communicators who have been trained by the Competition with female clients who bolster their delicate egos. The Competition's agents feel a sense of achievement when they are able to meet the emotional needs of these women. We need only to empower these female clients with the gift of seduction—Scraptus instructed you in various methods of its use—and watch nature take its course.

When the LCU manager's family disintegrates, so does his personal credibility. Occasionally you can push him over the edge, and he will move away with someone else's spouse. When that happens, little attention is paid to the so-called "message of light." Everybody in the LCU winds up focusing on damage control, condemnation, and expressions of outrage. This generally is coupled with the delightfully hypocritical "it wouldn't have happened to me" thinking.

Hotspur Memorandum Fourteen

To: flambeau@darkcorp.com
From: hotspur@darkcorp.com
Subject: The power of discouragement

I don't want you to leave this subject of diffusing the light without a mention of one of our best weapons against committed competition employees. I'm speaking of the matter of discouragement Paul gives a passing reference to in 2 Corinthians 4:1.

Flambeau, this is one of the most obvious and easy to use tools in our arsenal. It's so easy that even you should be able to master the technique.

Let me take you back to something you should have learned from my predecessor, Scraptus. Although he claimed credit for it, Scraptus actually learned the three levels of using discouragement, opposition, and intimidation from me. I'm inclined to agree with Scraptus that discouragement is one of the greatest resources developed by our Pernicious Founder to help rid the human race of joy. Remember, *joy* is a quality some humans develop that allows them to rise above their circumstances. Paul speaks of it frequently in the Philippians section of their corporate literature. Study it so you'll know how to diffuse and diminish it.

One of the best ways to spread discouragement and diminish joy is by the wise use of shame. Remember that we have already noted where Paul referred to it in 2 Corinthians 4:2. The Competition uses shame to cultivate an aversion to what they call "sinful practices"—the kind of behavior and even attitudes we promote in our corporate message. According to our research division, their corporate literature contains 104 references to shame. Study these references to understand their thinking.

Remember that shame always produces discouragement. Once I was assigned to a small local competition unit in the Western United States. The manager, my client, was an attractive, energetic human with a strong sense of what was morally right. I felt frustrated as I continually listened to his railing against moral sin. He made a big point of urging the females in his LCU to wear modest clothing. He even developed the habit of bringing a ruler to measure the length of the skirts of the young women.

That's when I came up with the idea of using a precocious teenager with a flair for the sensual to snare him. He couldn't believe what he found himself doing in response to her invitation! Neither could members of his LCU.

When a number of fellow corporate officers met with him over a period of time for accountability and encouragement, I continued hammering at him with the shame of what he had done. This kept him from participating in their restorative efforts or from pursuing reconciliation in his marriage.

Discouragement doesn't always have to be linked with shame. It can grow out of virtually any situation. Cultivate it among your clients, especially Gene. Remember the rules of discouragement:

- Always have your clients call attention to anything negative.
- Always distort each situation so that they think in the most negative terms.
- Prompt discouraging comments about any efforts at positive change. The "big three" are: (1) "That won't work"; (2) "We've already tried that"; and (3) "We've never done it that way."
- Don't forget non-verbal cues, such as rolling eyes, sighing, throwing hands up in despair.
- Remind clients of the importance of timing, inserting negative comments at just the point when conversation seems to be taking a positive turn.

Bottom line, Flambeau: Discouragement can be one of your greatest weapons for countering two of the Competition's strongest components in their arsenal—joy in the present and hope for the future. Make extensive use of it to remove them both.

Flambeau Memorandum Nine

To: hotspur@darkcorp.com
From: flambeau@darkcorp.com
Subject: But why be subtle?

I think I'm getting the point at which a form of limited mind-blinding can be effectively used even on those who will never return allegiance to our Master Below. But my question remains: Is subtlety really so crucial or are these championship shell games just excuses for bragging rights around the fire?

We've been assuming that any agent we want to subvert will resist. Frankly, there are a couple of people at Glencrest who would jump into our plans and do the breaststroke. I wish their personal demons would be a lot more aggressive in allowing them to help me out. These are much more experienced tempters, but they just seem to be setting these clients on a maintenance schedule, even though they are active in the LCU and hear the Business Plan continually. What makes them so safe?

In fact, the clients I'm thinking of hold management positions. But one of them seems more interested in using his LCU contacts to make his small retail store more popular. The other just likes to exert influence over people's lives—sort of like our CEO Below. These seem to be naturally deceitful and are wonderful light diffusers, but they could do more to subvert the "body" or at least to help me with Gene.

After all, legions of the competition's professional agents and ordinary representatives have been enticed by money, sex, or power to diffuse the "light." That's just good old demonic tempting with the basic vices.

Hotspur Memorandum Fifteen

To: flambeau@darkcorp.com
From: hotspur@darkcorp.com
Subject: Subtlety and deceit

You seem to be the one who's been standing in diffused light too long. First, why should these demons go out of their way to help you? You are the one on the spot at Glencrest. I've checked the database, and I think I see the two people you mean. One of them is a sleeper who already has helped sink two LCUs that were assigned to his demon.

I agree that these two have the potential to be of great service to you, but they won't work with the standard sins. You've failed to recognize the simple fact that their greatest value is to be hard-nosed naysayers. Their basic philosophy is that they will give the managers more than six inches of leash and wait to see what sort of trouble the LCU might get into. They are purse strings pullers and bean counters, as honest and moral as you will find among those humans. They can be our worst enemies if they are committed to the Competition and have a servant's heart. Try the straightforward no-subtlety tempting you prefer, and they'll just stomp on your head.

Treat them with subtlety, though, and you can play them like a fine cello. They can be our best allies if they are committed to running the LCU like a well-oiled business in which nobody gets out of line or practices the Competition's brand of spirituality. They walk about with a scowl and a signboard that says "Don't tread on me or mine." They have lots of integrity. Bitterness, fear of change, and the need to control blind them. We used to staff the boards of inquisition with just such people.

Of course, those with less integrity are susceptible to conventional sins. But they don't start out eager to do your bidding. You have to dance them toward the abyss. The vital component that can make this work is deceit. These agents—whether vocational managers or members of the non-vocational leadership team—must have come to the point at which they can justify their actions to themselves and are willing to go to great lengths to avoid having to justify themselves to others. They may even think they are hiding their indiscretions from their CEO Himself, which is the highest self-delusion.

Some time ago I attended a seminar on how to deal with integrity. As you may know, the Competition defines *integrity* as openness before their Master—not having deceit in their lives. You may find yourself better able to understand this concept if you go back to the place in the Business Plan where their VP Paul claimed that he and his colleagues "conducted themselves in the world in simplicity and godly sincerity" (2 Cor. 1:12). Careful examination of the terms he used shows us exactly where we need to concentrate our efforts. The term *simplicity* that Paul used has the idea of "no folds or wrinkles" in a garment. And the idea of "godly sincerity" is that of a pure motive.

If their corporate literature demands no hidden folds or wrinkles, then such flaws are provocative, both within individual clients such as Gene and especially with their LCU mangers and other corporate executives. We must never slack in our efforts to entice them into financial dishonesty, sexual impurity, or other deceitful thoughts and behaviors. Even a "secret corner of their minds" in which a manager entertains fantasies of sexual involvement with a woman in their LCU can be used. There's nothing like a little secret to blunt the sharp edge of integrity.

Some time ago a colleague blunted the integrity of one of his clients who helped manage his LCU and held an important job in one of their communications operations. The communication division was in the process of initiating changes in personnel. My colleague, Moretius, impressed on the mind of his client the importance of absolute secrecy in this matter, letting him dwell on the thought that we would benefit if word of this change leaked out. Moretius arranged for someone to ask the direct question, "Are you about to get rid of your spokesman and change to another?" Virtually without thinking, Moretius's client responded with an out-and-out lie. "Not at all," he replied. Later he felt he had been deceitful, but he never took any action. That incident opened a door to greater opportunities for deception in this man, and his personal integrity declined. The perception of integrity also declined as those to whom he lied learned that they could not always trust him.

I'll concede that we have been assuming that the agents we are attempting to subvert will resist initially. Of course, some are only in it to make money or exert influence over people. They are naturally deceitful and are wonderful light diffusers if they are resourceful enough to reach an important place in the competition's ministry without others finding out what they are like.

Their Business Plan labels this "peddling the Word of God" (2 Cor. 2:17). I came up with the original idea of inserting these sleeper agents into important and highly visible responsibilities after convincing them that they could "make it in the religion racket." After all, we've always been in the business of peddling some variety of their message. Who's to say they can't do this as well? When I presented the idea to Low Command, they bought it immediately.

I'm particularly proud to have developed one refinement in deceit for financial gain—a manual on how the Competition's leaders can use their service to avoid governmental tax liability. You may recall their CEO's Son once gave instruction to "render to Caesar the things that are Caesar's, and to God the things that are God's" (Matt. 22:21 BP). My manual includes specific directions on how to initiate thinking that subverts both of these stated objectives.

For example, I strongly urge adopting the rationale that people in "God's service" make less money. Therefore they ought to be paid in cash or without the keeping of records, so they won't have to pay taxes on the funds they receive. Flambeau, I can't tell you how many LCUs have diminished their light by engaging in this practice. I'm sure you can see how this generates a hole in their integrity. My manual also explains the tactic of convincing them that they need not give anything financially to support the LCU, since they are giving their very lives to their CEO's work.

As a result of this communication strategy, a significant number of vocational LCU managers have never given a nickel to their operations. It's a form of rationalization, and one of its side benefits is that it encourages pride—another thing their Business Plan warns them not to do (Rom. 12:3).

Let me repeat for your limited understanding, Flambeau, that legions of their professional agents and ordinary representatives have been enticed by money, sex, or power to diffuse the "light." That's why you need to continue to develop and use these basic vices as a part of your arsenal of weapons.

Strategic Initiative Three: Joint Ventures

> O Corinthians! We have spoken openly to you, our heart is wide open. You are not restricted by us, but you are restricted by your own affections. Now in return for the same (I speak as to children), you also be open.

Do not be unequally yoked together with unbelievers. For what fellowship has righteousness with lawlessness? And what communion has light with darkness? And what accord has Christ with Belial? Or what part has a believer with an unbeliever? And what agreement has the temple of God with idols? For you are the temple of the living God. As God has said:

> "I will dwell in them
> and walk among them.
> I will be their God,
> And they shall be My people."

Therefore

> "Come out from among them
> And be separate, says the Lord.
> Do not touch what is unclean,
> And I will receive you."
> "I will be a Father to you,
> And you shall be My sons and daughters,
> Says the LORD Almighty."

Therefore, having these promises, beloved, let us cleanse ourselves from all filthiness of the flesh and spirit, perfecting holiness in the fear of God. (2 Cor. 6:11–7:1 BP)

Flambeau Memorandum Ten

To: hotspur@darkcorp.com
From: flambeau@darkcorp.com
Subject: The power of freedom

I must admit that sometimes I find these assignments mind-numbing. I understand that there is value to studying this propaganda, but it would seem more beneficial to consider our own perspectives on our CEO Below, our business plan, and the tactics Low Command has developed for takeovers, acquisitions, and corporate buyouts. Is it really that valuable to spend so much time poring over the Competition's Business Plan?

But, since we had such a strong presence in Corinth, I can see some value in understanding what concerned the Competition's leadership team regarding our very profitable operation in that part of their wretched planet.

From the segment I'm currently considering, it seems evident that their vice president Paul had become obsessed with fears about links between their assets and ours (2 Cor. 6:14–18 BP). While their corporate agenda differs radically from the objectives of our business, one would think they might at least occasionally be open to mutually beneficial joint activities. But what Paul wrote precluded any marriages or close business arrangements or joint causes for the good of the species. His comments about being "unequally yoked together" are an insult to our corporate presence; he implies no commonality whatsoever.

This would seem to be an issue of personal freedom. After all, the Competition supposedly offers freedom in their CEO's Son. Freedom also is our stock in trade, the most valuable commodity we have to offer. Paul seems only to want these wretched clients to give mind-numbing allegiance to his agenda, without even the chance to try out ours. If he's so interested in liberty, why does he not encourage association with our people so the little gerbils can make up their own minds?

It seems the central focus of our marketing plan should be on the freedom we afford when they sign on with us. No, I am not forgetting that our freedom is only hype. We have every intention of enslaving them to the Top Guy Down Below. But it seems at times that the Competition is just as serious about clamping on the chains. At times they even say so up front, which sounds ridiculous.

I'm thinking we need to point out the similarities between the Competition's tender offer and ours. Minimize the differences. Maximize through the presentation of joint venture offers what in essence appears to be a great business opportunity for them, but which in reality will serve our own purposes.

Hotspur Memorandum Sixteen

To: flambeau@darkcorp.com
From: hotspur@darkcorp.com
Subject: The emphasis on reconciliation

It seems clear to me that you don't seem to be taking into account the intensity of their efforts against us. Intensity in itself isn't necessarily an asset. However, well directed intensity can level the playing field. This is one reason I find it helpful to study our plans from their perspective.

To understand the issue of joint ventures as the Competition discusses them in 2 Corinthians 6:14–18, you need to back up a paragraph or two in the Business Plan to understand how intensely Paul felt about the larger subject.

Paul considered that the most important thing in his existence was the fact that he had been recruited out of our association and into a close, intimate connection with the Competition's CEO. He considered that the CEO's Son successfully carried out the infamous sneak attack on our position at great cost to Himself. As unfortunate and unfair as was this incursion into our world, I have to admit that Paul surely was right about the cost to the CEO and His Son.

Paul's life and this "ministry of reconciliation" he mentioned in 5:18 were paid for at such a high price that freedom becomes irrelevant. Whenever anyone has that kind of understanding of our horrible miscalculation, he or she has irrevocably crossed the line into service. We can manipulate them to misuse their zeal occasionally, but we can never fully win them back.

This section about believers and unbelievers being yoked together goes way beyond simple affiliations, in the mind of Paul.

He knew that a lot of the Corinthians were delightfully close to our turf. So it is with our clients today. We still can snatch them away, and they will have lost the opportunity purchased for them. Unfortunately, in the case of the Corinthians, Paul used his intensity on the issue to direct them away from these most beneficial relationships so that not one life he touched would end up joined to His Debased Majesty.

Keep in mind that Paul knew, just as you do, how we intend to use every connection between our assets and those who are not beyond our recovery. Do you still wonder why he is obsessed over this issue? Had I been in his sandals, I would have been as well.

This great cost is the core of what Paul meant by "the ministry of reconciliation." Their corporate message is the "word of reconciliation" (2 Cor. 5:19). He was an "ambassador" of reconciliation for their Founder's Son and spoke directly for their Founder as a "worker together" with His Son—applying the reconciliation that the CEO's misguided notion of mercy has cost.

That urgent intensity has cost us more than a few sales, Flambeau.

This is another case where their athletic contests mimic the pathetic lives of humans. I'm thinking of something that happened in the sport of American-style football. One year a single college team so dominated the contests they played that everyone assumed that they were the best. They had the most talented players and the most savvy coaches. This powerhouse team was called the Seminoles from a university in Florida. They were so good that it seemed a waste of time even to arrange games to determine the top team in the United States. They were smart, talented, arrogant, resourceful, and intimidating.

But there was another team from Oklahoma called the Sooners. They were good as well, and in a normal year heads would have turned their way. But this year the team from Florida had eclipsed them.

The Sooner coach was a masterful motivator and manipulator. He understood that the one best thing he had going for him in the final playoff game against the Seminoles was the fact that nobody thought his boys belonged on the same field.

He whipped his troops into a fevered pitch, pounding into their minds the message that "nobody believes we can do it—but we can, if we want it badly enough."

When sheer ability met sheer fire on the playing field, it was fire that prevailed. The Seminoles were overconfident because they underestimated the power of their opponents' intensity.

We dare not underestimate the efforts of fanatics such as Paul. These puny little humans do not belong on the same field with us. But there is no way in which we can match the motivation of this reconciliation theology, so it is hard to match their intensity.

The Sooners played with great ability. Paul's team was a lot rougher. The only things the message of reconciliation has going for it are the presence of the CEO in the team and the intensity that the message stirs in the players. However, we dare not underestimate those two factors.

Low Command spent a great deal of time studying this issue. The ignoble mucky-mucks finally concluded that one way to prevent their agents from becoming intense, successful recruiters is to engage them in other kinds of activities like those you suggest. Once we cut them out of the herd and get them in partnership with our agents, we can play with their loyalties and priorities. They may be motivated by a desire to influence our agents. It rarely happens. We will influence them a lot more often. But the best thing we can do is to destroy their intensity.

Flambeau Memorandum Eleven

To: hotspur@darkcorp.com
From: flambeau@darkcorp.com
Subject: The issue of strength

One thing I was hoping you would explain to me is what exactly Paul meant in 2 Corinthians 6:14 regarding this "yoke." I notice some versions call it "bound together," but that seems only a little helpful.

I now have learned that in Paul's time a yoke was a wooden device that fit over the necks of animals so that their strong chests and shoulders could be used to pull a heavy load or wrestle a plow or harrow over a field.

I assume that Paul is being metaphorical instead of literal here, but I still wonder what is meant by Paul's comments. I would like to think that some of our people are every bit as spiritual as the other side's. The spirituality just has a different object.

I suppose we are more likely to successfully blunt their recruiting efforts when we acheive close proximity.

Hotspur Memorandum Seventeen

To: flambeau@darkcorp.com
From: hotspur@darkcorp.com
Subject: Yokes and giants

I'm sure you remember from the historical section of their Business Plan how we had some limited success in frightening the cowardly Israelites (Num. 13:27–14:23). But we found the limits of that tactic with our oversized agent Goliath (1 Sam. 17).

There is, however, a tangential matter that Scraptus brought up with you, one which should be repeated. Any time we can draw one of their agents into close relation with our world, we have the potential to intimidate. Occasionally intimidation can be physical. When the country of Saudi Arabia began taking in a lot of oil dollars they began sending a great many of their best and brightest young men to Western universities. That put them within reach of the Competition and was worrisome until we worked out a simple countermeasure. Before they left, the students were told that if they made any changes in religion overseas they would be shot upon their return. We had little trouble after that.

Remember that intimidation is an effective weapon against the LCU and its leaders when it results in discouragement, as noted above. Intimidation can be applied in a number of ways, from inside the LCU and from outside. Just now we are talking about it in relation to yoking a believer in an intimidating outside relationship.

As I already suggested, Goliath was a failure at intimidation, but at the same time a different sort of intimidation proved more successful in destabilizing the nation that the Competition's CEO was trying to put together. We subverted the first manager of Israeli operations, Saul, who had been hired even though he had never played much of a role in their operations. We capitalized on what we considered a strategic error by their CEO by intimidating Saul with our view of power.

For example, Saul knew that people followed successful fighters. So when a shrimp kid named David took out our giant agent Goliath—whom Saul had feared to face—Saul figured that David would soon take his job, and all the heads in his family would soon be separated from their respective bodies. David had no such intention, but Saul was intimidated by his connections and sought to implement the usual solution to such problems—neutralize the potential threat.

As usual, the Competition's goal was to place a leader over their national enterprise who did not operate like our managers at that level. They wanted someone who would place total reliance in their CEO. So, ironically, what Saul most feared eventually happened—he and most of his family were wiped out and David claimed the throne. But it didn't happen for the reason he feared. He was intimidated into destroying himself.

Before I leave my brief history lesson, Flambeau, I want to point out that intimidation almost brought down one of the Competition's committed executives. We nearly managed to manipulate the same David who had shut down our Philistine operative.

Pharlus had a client named Nabal who was especially proficient at verbal intimidation. Let me explain Nabal's excellent technique. It should serve as a template for using intimidation today. You will find it in the Competition's Business Plan at 1 Samuel 25:10–11.

First, he questioned David's value. "Who is David, and who is the son of Jesse?" he asked David's servants. None of these pathetic humans likes to be thought of as a nobody. Frequently when you diminish their personal value, they'll respond just to show you that they do matter.

Nabal's second strategy was to lump David into a category of lowlifes. "There are many servants nowadays who break away each one from his master." In other words, David fit into one of the classes of common criminals. The world would be better off if Saul caught and punished this ordinary ruffian.

The third strategy of Nabal was to imply that David and his people couldn't be trusted: "Shall I then take my bread and my water and my meat that I've killed for my shearers, and give it to men when I do not know where they are from?" Of course he knew who these men were and where they were from, but he dismissed them as wandering beggars and David as the chief bum.

David's representatives turned on their heels, went back to their leader, and relayed all the words of Nabal. David's response was exactly as Pharlus planned. Without considering the implications, David ordered his men to get their swords and kill Nabal and everyone associated with him. That would have destroyed his effectiveness as a leader of compassionate integrity. He would have been forever branded as a person who used our methods to gain respect.

However, Pharlus had not accounted for the fact that the Competition had their own agent in place—Abigail, Nabal's wife. She intercepted David and his troops and bribed them, giving him a chance to regain perspective.

Pharlus did a good job of cultivating his client Nabal, but he failed to watch out for corporate espionage. It only takes one wise agent to refocus the committed agent back onto their CEO, neutralizing our effort.

So, when you try intimidation or any other strategy, Flambeau, watch your backside. They often have agents where we would not expect to find them.

Suppose Pharlus had succeeded. David would have gone from intimidated to intimidator. There have been some excellent examples of that working, either with their agents or those who purport to represent them. Either way, when they adopt our tactics, the force of their message spins off-course. Look at what we accomplished with those wars of territorial conquest known as the Crusades. Most of the soldiers who went off to those wars were our agents, but those who were not were drawn in by intimidating fears and prejudices. And they all went out under the Competition's corporate logo, so their message came into disrepute either way.

Flambeau Memorandum Twelve

To: hotspur@darkcorp.com
From: flambeau@darkcorp.com
Subject: Yokes. Remember?

I found your previous e-mail on intimidation interesting and informative. Nevertheless, what I was asking about was the significance of the *yoke* in Paul's argument, not so much whether he was talking about physical strength and intimidation.

Scraptus said you sometimes have a problem with focus.

What I am most concerned about is how far we should go to avoid unhealthy relationships between our people and theirs. Is it hazardous for our affiliates to associate with the Competition? After all, they are out to recruit our people. I've seen their successes among the members of the local franchise at Glencrest. In fact, I once sent an operative in to work undercover to disrupt a "discipling program." Our man professed to be signing on with them, then began working through the program with the idea of recruiting for us.

Unfortunately, his contact led to a successful takeover on their part. So perhaps their vice president may share some of the same concerns we should have. I'm awaiting your thoughts on the hazards of associating with the Competition.

Hotspur Memorandum Eighteen

To: flambeau@darkcorp.com
From: hotspur@darkcorp.com
Subject: Mixing apples and wax bananas

I suppose I assumed, mistakenly as it turns out, that you can figure out for yourself the obvious things. All right, let me "focus" on the matter of the "yoke."

Haven't you ever had a client who worked in farming before the days of mechanization? If farmers hitched a draft horse and a donkey in the same hitch, plowing a field or planting a crop could be impossible. The strong, large animal would wear out doing all the plowing, and the small animal would wear himself out straining in the only direction possible—sideways, fighting against the direction the stronger animal was headed. The nature of harness is that if you do not have fairly evenly matched animals, you are better off using only one, or they will angle off toward nowhere. The ancient wooden oxen yoke was even worse if animals were unsuitably paired for size and strength.

The principle of separation was vital to the early operation of the Competition's Business Plan. There were ethical implications that Paul was highlighting, as well as matters of appropriate assignment of roles.

Does one put two kinds of grapes side by side in the same vineyard? No, because they will cross-pollinate and a third, wild strain will emerge which will defile the vineyard (Deut. 22:9 BP).

Does one plow with an ox and a donkey yoked together? No, because your work will be frustrated and defiled (v. 10).

Does one mix wool and linen in the same garment? No, the wool will give more than the flax strands, and the garment will fall apart (v. 11).

For the same reason, they were to sew tassels onto their clothing to remind them to stay yoked in prayer so they would not be defiled (v. 12). And they were to make sure that their marriage relationships were pure, not unequally yoked and so defiled (22:13–24:5).

See how the practical moves to the ethical, on which there is a whole lot to say about the yoke of sexual purity and marriage? Paul was speaking to many who would pick up on his allusions to these rules immediately. The connections between the yoke and combining things that don't belong together and defilement had been pounded into the thinking of these followers of their CEO.

The Competition often referred to these as "laws of separation." There were other such laws. Their aim was to make the people very wary about any joint venture with us. Their CEO knows that one of our favorite strategies is to put together projects that seem to advance their purposes but that really only promote our agenda.

A standard countermeasure at times when the Competition is successfully recruiting has been to activate sleeper agents in their management teams. These agents appeal to what the Competition would consider legitimate compassionate concerns. The goal is to siphon off energy and emphasis from their message to these new emphases. Message-centered recruiting goals are minimized so that the LCUs can become more inclusive. It gets them every time.

One of our most fruitful ventures of the last century was called the Ecumenical Movement. It is still in use, though it may be more generically described as "intercommunion dialogue" or something similarly warm and fuzzy. It's a marvelous technique, Flambeau, and it has potential as part of your strategy for advancing our cause at Glencrest. It also is quite versatile, with applications both at individual LCUs and at higher levels of the corporate organization.

We even developed national and international "councils" where dialogue occurs among all sorts of groups, theirs and ours. Over the years these councils have been so effective in our takeover strategy that most of the bodies with strong ties to these councils are now mostly ours. The Competition's affiliates believe they are achieving noble causes that will make the CEO's Son (or some version of Him) relevant around the globe. Most of the time these enterprises do far more to further our corporate mission than theirs.

Much of the pioneering work in this movement occurred in England during the late 1800s. It was sometimes referred to as the "down-grade controversy." In those days the Competition referred to some business units as "nonconformist." It was a time when we were successfully infiltrating or neutralizing major national affiliates of the Competition. The nonconformists had given us more trouble, because they refused to be part of the more pliable big organizations.

One of their most effective nonconformists was a marketing professional named Charles Spurgeon, who was one of the first to identify our strategy. He identified three corporate trends among the LCUs:

First, "a general unwillingness to define doctrinal issues precisely . . . and unwillingness to question the beliefs of any . . . in the name of Christian charity." In other words, they had watered down the core corporate values and anyone who complained was put down as unloving.

Second, the Business Plan was no longer followed as the final authority.

Third, they replaced the desire to find what was true with the desire to find what things worked.

Spurgeon screamed that LCUs would cease to be authentic competition affiliates if the attacks were allowed to continue. They were, in fact, part of a new religion that was too dishonest to admit that it was no longer the old. People were unfed, so they were tired of these LCU's devotional meetings and ready for entertainment instead. They were connected to the "unholy" and "many would like to unite church and stage, cards and prayer, dancing and sacraments." They had invented their own teachings to fit what they wanted to hear.

"Avowed atheists are not a tenth as dangerous as those preachers who scatter doubt midst avid faith," Spurgeon said. "Skepticism . . . has flashed from the pulpit and spread among the people."

Flambeau, I've summarized what we learned from this intercepted Competition document to show you how effective we were.

Just keep remembering our version of their vice president's line: "Yoke our people to believers at every opportunity."

Flambeau Memorandum Thirteen

To: hotspur@darkcorp.com
From: flambeau@darkcorp.com
Subject: So why doesn't it work?

I always wonder about the sincerity of you upper-level demons in your advice. I guess I can understand what you mean about getting my clients connected to the "right" sorts of people. But if the strategy hits a snag, who gets blamed for it, with threats of flailing, barbecuing, or trips to the North Pole? No, not you. I wind up taking all the heat here, so to speak.

I know you have said I shouldn't let our people wander into their recruiting meetings. So should I have done anything differently when I lost our operative to the discipleship group? Are there parameters in this yoke business, so that I don't lose any body parts in retribution?

Hotspur Memorandum Nineteen

To: flambeau@darkcorp.com
From: hotspur@darkcorp.com
Subject: Back to the ABCs

I am surprised, Flambeau, to hear your whining, as if we should somehow appreciate your feeble failures. You should have learned long ago that there are consequences if you lose a client. You tried to yoke one of our operatives to their strongest type of recruitment group, and then you wonder what happened when they recruited him? Don't even try to elicit my sympathy on that one, you flaming idiot.

All right. Let me try to be basic enough so you can understand what we are after in unequal yoking. Think back to our first success in the competition for clients. The Bottom Guy's tactic was to get that first human couple to act independently of their CEO. He distracted the woman with the possibility that she could have something that was being denied to her because their CEO was selfish. She bought the line that if she could understand good and evil, she would be like their CEO, and He was selfish and wanted to deprive her.

Yes, she showed even less brainpower than you did, but she didn't know any better. She was starting to think with her senses, her desire for pleasure, and her ego interest in knowledge without paying the price of discipline to get it.

What was really attractive was the chance for those first two miserable humans to be their own CEOs.

That's always been our aim. That's why the Competition has to keep urging their people to keep unstained from the world (James 1:27; 4:4 BP). Our job is to emphasize the priority of "number one." We've been fairly successful at this. Self-actualization, self-fulfillment, self-realization are common human themes in the Western world. We've also successfully blurred the distinction between our two corporate entities. That's why their VP Paul was so insistent about the "unequal yoke." They are an absolute bottom priority for us, so long as we can keep cutting them from the herd and bringing them into the world of the sensual self. Got that? They come to us, or we send an operative to take our case to them at their weakest point, the herd. Don't ever willingly place one of our people in a functioning, strong small group study again!

Asinine dunderhead! Cretan! Blithering fool!

Several hours have passed, and I think I have regained composure. Where was I?

The most successful way to promote unequal yokes is to lure their people into a marriage to one of our clients. There is no better way to neutralize a committed agent than through such a liaison. The standard line to use with their clients is that "I know she's not a Christian, but she's the only woman I've ever met who has the kind of interest in the outdoors I have, who enjoys the same music I do, who even thinks like me. I'm sure we can overcome our religious differences." Better yet: "I'm sure that he is almost ready to come to the Lord. It won't be long once we are married." They actually delude themselves into thinking that it works like that, because they know what they have decided to do and now want to put a sanctified spin on it. Lust and loneliness . . . what wonderful tools.

This brings us to your opportunities, Flambeau. Why haven't you sought to employ this strategy with Gene? His wife died, and he became one of the Competition's recruits through one of their members of the opposite sex. Obviously he is susceptible to being enticed that way. Why haven't you directed one of our female assets into contact with him, and sought to bring about a marriage?

Better yet, a "live-in arrangement" while they see if they are compatible . . . recently that has become a practical and attractive option for us to suggest with their agents.

The other place you should use the unequally yoked strategy is in business. Mixed working environments can be mildly pleasing, but what really brings results is an out-and-out partnership, preferably with signed contractual partner-partner arrangements. I hope you realize that all of this is at the preschool level of tempter knowledge, but after your last e-mail I'm wondering if you shouldn't go back for a refresher in burning sandbox.

We've already begun using the corporate version of unequal yokes. It is oh, so satisfying to see one of their national LCU organizations standing at the ecumenical altar with a group we have owned for most of a century. I don't often cry at weddings, but . . .

I recently learned of an organization with close affiliations to the Competition's corporate objectives that had begun using the Internet to promote their values and objectives. A couple of our key affiliates have worked with them to include a division in which they were promoting organized gambling. Open-mindedness is such a wondrous invention.

Strategic Initiative Four: Waging War

> Now I, Paul, myself am pleading with you by the meekness and gentleness of Christ—who in presence am lowly among you, but being absent am bold toward you. But I beg you that when I am present I may not be bold with that confidence by which I intend to be bold against some, who think of us as if we walked according to the flesh.

For though we walk in the flesh, we do not war according to the flesh. For the weapons of our warfare are not carnal but mighty in God for pulling down strongholds, casting down arguments and every high thing that exalts itself against the knowledge of God, bringing every thought into captivity to the obedience of Christ, and being ready to punish all disobedience when your obedience is fulfilled. (2 Cor. 10:1–6 BP)

Flambeau Memorandum Fourteen

To: hotspur@darkcorp.com
From: flambeau@darkcorp.com
Subject: Meek warriors and captive thinking

I am not quite so dense as to have forgotten about the value of mixed business and marriage partnerships. But I'd like to set that aside and move on to the next subject of capturing thoughts and warfare found in the 2 Corinthians section of the Competition's Business Plan.

I located VP Paul's next references to our Enterprising Founder in 10:1–6. Though our Founder isn't mentioned explicitly, Paul speaks of warfare for the mind in a way that can only refer to our ongoing feud. I've read that every business plan should identify the competition. Paul appears to acknowledge here that we are their chief competitor, and that we have seriously disparate interests.

From Low Command, I've heard much about the danger of this concept of meekness and gentleness, which their vice president refers to as describing himself. I have no idea what this is all about. Is it the same thing as weakness? Somehow I've gotten the impression it's something our Infernal Founder would repudiate in a human heartbeat. After all, there was nothing weak about his "grand entrance" into the Competition's corporate headquarters.

I notice that Paul says that this "meekness and gentleness" comes from their CEO's Son. At times He seemed neither meek nor gentle. After all, He proved to be a stubborn adversary to our Debased Founder in what their manual refers to as the "Temptation" in Matthew 4:4, 7, 10. He frequently seemed to exhibit a confrontational touch as He challenged our agents. He flashed anger and spoke harsh words.

Look at the "meek and gentle" way He drove the merchandis-ers from their commerce center in the temple (Mark 11:15–18 BP). I understand He actually became physically violent, using a whip, overturning tables, and refusing to permit anyone to carry merchandise through. It just puzzles me how He could describe himself as "meek and lowly in heart" (Matt. 11:28–29 BP) with that sort of temper.

For another thing, how could a meek person possibly pose a threat to our corporate initiatives? I think we ought to concede this particular trait to the Competition and encourage them to in-stall it in the minds of all their clients. Surely it will weaken them.

This meekness and gentleness reference seems especially odd at this point in Paul's message since he moves from it into mili-tary language. I understand that war to them was a major deal. Their Hebrew division couldn't seem to get enough of it, sending many souls into our welcoming arms. From the time they entered "the promised land" until the Roman legions kicked them out of the land for good after the Bar Kokhba Rebellion—about a cen-tury after the CEO's Son was there—they were usually fighting somebody or other.

Since he was a citizen of Rome, which knew a thing or two about winning wars, Paul must have been aware of military struc-ture. We made sure he found out a lot more about it as a govern-ment prisoner. Warfare and weapons played a role in what he sought to communicate to his clients.

Apparently they view us as more than just competitors. I know there is a significant struggle between us for the control of human assets. You've certainly nagged me enough about how important it is for us to develop effective defensive strategies to rebuff their initiatives.

Is that what the Competition has in mind here? I find it odd that he moves from an aside about "the meekness and gentleness of Christ" into this allusion to warring according to the flesh and according to the spirit. He certainly doesn't seem to be interested in just holding old ground, since he wants to use these spiritual weapons to breach fortresses. That would be our fortresses, wouldn't it? Yet he is not talking about taking human prisoners for the CEO as we do, but thoughts.

How does one take a thought captive?

Hotspur Memorandum Twenty

To: flambeau@darkcorp.com
From: hotspur@darkcorp.com
Subject: Military relations

As I mentioned, I was pleased that you could spot this subtle allusion to the CEO Below so readily. Many of your demonic predecessors overlooked this portion—to their great loss, for these are not insignificant matters.

You've also done well in identifying the issues as a warfare of thoughts and raising questions about meekness, but you've also badly missed the point about meekness. However, this is a common error. Demons usually take just the attitude you voice, which is why Low Command issues so many directives about its dangers. Humans walking through rugged places on earth occasionally die because they do not notice a viper sunning itself along the path. When you think of meekness and lowliness, think of that deadly snake lying quietly in the sun.

You understand the concept of warfare. Our Enterprising Founder prides himself on being "at war" with the Competition. Never forget that our corporate competition is a war of extreme proportions. Our leader has expressed an intention to carry out a successful takeover campaign. He has already succeeded in a series of hostile takeovers. In the Western division, to which you have been assigned, Europe and North America have been a battleground on which we have seen spectacular gains. You will remember that this area was once the scene of a bloody guerrilla campaign of recruiting drives and world takeover plots that went under the name of "cross-cultural missions." It was a frightening and intense conflagration. More recently we have seen success at every level in this region, from education and government to entertainment, business, and commerce. I've already mentioned our corporate takeovers through ecumenism.

However, you must understand the fact that we consider ourselves at war against the Competition doesn't mean that everything we do takes on the nature of out-and-out warfare. All you have to do is run the numbers, Flambeau. Understand that they control two-thirds of the angelic assets, while we can only count on one-third (see Revelation 12:4 in their BP). For this reason, we can only initiate conflict with ambushes and terroristic raids at points of our choosing. But these are quite effective, both in human business and warfare. Sometimes we initiate a reign of terror, making use of intimidation and fear.

At other times, as we have already discussed, our approach is more subtly nuanced and manipulative. After all, our Enterprising Founder is nothing if not the master of deceit. You'll learn more about this in the next portion of our Competition's Business Plan.

Let me start here with your question about meekness. The best human soldiers are picked out to receive a training so harsh that only a small number of them get through it. This "special forces" training has three aims. First, the soldiers are taught to be ferocious and lethal fighters. Second, they learn how to blend in with the surrounding terrain so well that they move silently and invisibly. Third, they learn to function as a team rather than individuals. Theirs is a self-confident, bold, self-denying meekness.

Paul never would have stood out in a contest of forceful personalities. He wasn't much to look at and had a demeanor of a scholar. His boldness came in his words, especially words written in the power of the presence of his CEO. His meekness was taken as weakness by some in Corinth. He didn't seem to have anything with which to back up his strong words.

Our agents quickly learned that Paul was a spiritual special forces fighter, who was prepared to direct his arguments and spiritual authority with violent effect against us whenever we crossed him.

We have succeeded in infiltrating their units with forceful and praise-winning personalities at every level. But this meek boldness is not something we've ever been able to reproduce with much success. There is a quality there that only the Competition knows how to reproduce. It's a character trait that is hard to describe, except to say that it is like that of the CEO's Son.

Whenever you identify that kind of meekness, evacuate your client from the vicinity immediately. You are staring lethal power in the face.

Flambeau Memorandum Fifteen

To: hotspur@darkcorp.com
From: flambeau@darkcorp.com
Subject: War tactics

I am beginning to understand why the Competition's CEO's Son made that statement about the meek "inheriting the earth."

Perhaps that begins to address another issue I find difficult to understand. Their corporate literature places so much importance on the mind. Here Paul talks about capturing arguments, knowledge, and thoughts; so I assume the human mind is more than simply our primary arena of competition.

I've had some success working on Gene's mind, convincing him that he shouldn't feel secure in his newly established alliance with the Competition's local franchise at Glencrest. I've been telling him that he shouldn't take literally our Competitor's propaganda that he has some kind of personal relationship with their Founder's Son. I've been repeating to him how ludicrous it is to believe that their Top Executive would have any kind of personal interest in him. Everyone knows that big corporations are out to exploit the little guy. Sometimes I think he's paying attention to me, but at other times I suspect they have developed some sophisticated communications technique that neutralizes my best efforts.

I'm sure you'll underscore the importance of continuing to bombard my clients with our agenda while seeking to neutralize the Competition's corporate mission, vision, and values.

Another issue is Paul's discussion about walking according to the flesh. I was intrigued by his statement, "For though we walk in the flesh, we do not war according to the flesh" (2 Cor. 10:3

BP). I've been led to believe that a big part of our strategy is to cause them to succumb to their flesh; things like sexual indiscretions, alcohol and drug abuse, overeating, and other forms of sensuality. So while I understand the seat of these issues lies in the mind, a lot of our work seems to take place in the realm of the flesh.

Hotspur Memorandum Twenty-One

To: flambeau@darkcorp.com
From: hotspur@darkcorp.com
Subject: Tactical matters—the shield of sarcasm

You raise issues that are best answered with another portion of their Business Plan, the sixth chapter of Ephesians (vv. 10–17). Here the same VP who wrote to the Corinthians offers a suit of virtual armor to enable them to stand against our CEO's strategies. Over and over, Paul used the word *stand*, trying to encourage these weak, vacillating followers not to turn tail and run as they are so prone to do when we attack them.

These weapons seem archaic by today's standards, but the Competition's clients are continually being directed to study the belt and breastplate and such, so they must be taking some understanding from it. His Lowness took the description seriously enough that he immediately ordered a committee to analyze the implications of these allusions to armor and weapons and come up with countermeasures, our own "weapons of warfare." Surely you have studied these before. Their importance should not be underestimated.

I recommend that you start with the shield of sarcasm. You may recall from your contacts with your former mentor, Scraptus, that sarcasm involves pointed humor laced with anger. There is, in fact, a carefully camouflaged intent to harm. Perhaps you remember, though I doubt it, that Scraptus likened sarcasm to a sniper's rifle. While that analogy has some conceptual accuracy, I would encourage you to think of sarcasm as a shield, protecting the soul from expressions of love, compassion, and concern that the Competition's people throw about. Love is one of the

Competition's stock products, and it is like meekness in that it poses a grave but unseen danger to our clients.

This love, and all the other weapons of the Competition must be countered in the mind, you will observe. I hope you begin to see the answer to your question. We spend a lot of time maneuvering physical temptations and seductions through the senses. But short of tying a client down and physically forcing some sin down his throat (which would not count even if we could do it), there are always choices about physical things. It is only in the mind that we can maneuver the person to think his choices are restricted or to educate the affections so they become powerful motivators.

In other words, we always do our physical thing for emotional/spiritual reasons. All of the battle ultimately takes place in the mind, however physical the temptations.

These humans are crazed for love, Flambeau. They just can't get enough of it, though they aren't nearly so ready to give it out to others. The Competition really loves the little slimeballs. And their agents are taught to love one another to a fault, even the ones who are least lovable. A small dose of sarcasm, inserted at strategic points out of an underlying envy, an unresolved lack of forgiveness, or just the desire to be humorous, can throw a lot of love straight into the garbage. Equip your clients to use it, and it will earn great dividends in warding off tendencies to give love and the disgusting results of receiving it.

Flambeau Memorandum Sixteen

To: hotspur@darkcorp.com
From: flambeau@darkcorp.com
Subject: Sarcasm and humor

Reading your last communication, it occurs to me that sarcasm is one of the tools that most mimics our own pattern of operation. Our Boss's first question with the human woman was a sarcastic statement: "Has God really said that you can't do what we all know you want to do? . . . Yeah, right." Sarcasm immediately showed our lack of respect toward their CEO, and it infected the woman. She made a lame attempt to represent God's position, immediately exaggerating what He had told her. Her latent resentment was apparent, and his Heinous Lowness jumped in with a frontal assault on the goodness of their Founder.

Sarcasm also was our ploy in designing the very first temptation aimed at the CEO's son (Matt. 4:2 BP). "If you are such hot stuff, and you are really hungry, turn rocks into bread."

Wow, I had not noticed before that this was precisely the same temptation. You can prove yourself with just a nibble. Only this time the target didn't "bite." In fact, the Business Plan quotation He came up with did answer the challenge posed to the CEO's Son. It just deflected the issue toward the Business Plan as the source.

I noticed as well that the CEO's Son used humor a lot in talking to people. He made jokes at the expense of our top sales staff at the time. But I can find no instance of His using true sarcasm. Perhaps that is significant.

Hotspur Memorandum Twenty-Two

To: flambeau@darkcorp.com
From: hotspur@darkcorp.com
Subject: Tactical matters and our armor

You made a couple of good observations about sarcasm. Just don't get bogged down in the nuances and miss the main point. I'm saying that sarcasm is a shield because it separates the individual client from others. Maintaining separation—keeping individuals away from the herd—makes them vulnerable.

True, we use sarcasm as an offensive weapon. But if you can keep resentments percolating and bubbling into interactions with others, sarcasm becomes a defensive weapon from your client's perspective—keeping others at arm's length by stinging them if they get too close.

Now, back to the armory.

The second defensive weapon to put on your clients is the belt of arrogance, by which we will counter the damaging blows of meekness to the midsection. The soldier's belt protected the belly and kept extraneous clothing from getting in the way or tripping the fighter at inopportune moments. This belt keeps clients from tripping over the truth about themselves.

Remember, Flambeau, the Competition places great importance on humility. We simply cannot allow our clients to be humble or they will become meek and lowly like the CEO's Son. Use every variety of arrogance liberally. Convince Gene and your other clients that they are always right—especially when they're wrong. Being proven wrong or weak is a blow to our carefully instilled self-indulgent egolatry.

Keep in mind that we are never to be deterred from our

objectives by truth. Whether something is true is irrelevant. The question is, does it puff up the person's ego? If so, then truth is grand self-deception. A positive truth affirms what the client most wants to believe about himself. A negative truth makes her defensive. Substituting the word *lie* for *truth* makes not a whit of difference in this regard. Our CEO Below is proud to be the "Father of lies." A truth hog-tied with the rope of self is the best lie.

Convince your clients that, whatever their financial or marital or interpersonal difficulties, no fault lies with them. They are in trouble because of circumstance or upbringing or genetics, or spouse. Since they have the natural tendency to want to be their own CEO, they will eat up this defense of themselves like smooth chocolate pudding. That's the value of the belt of arrogance, Flambeau—it supports pride, which makes a lie truth and truth a lie. It keeps the truth of their CEO, which we can't really subvert, tucked neatly out of the way.

Third, they should wear the breastplate of indifference. Like the shield of sarcasm, it's a protective device. Weak, tender affections bounce right off. Warm thoughts from inside the person can't get out to cause us problems. We want our clients to be, as Paul said, "past feeling" (Eph. 4:19 BP). That's exactly what we have in mind here, Flambeau—a tough scale of indifference so the Competition can't massage warmth into a cold heart. The desire for "self-preservation" which was designed into these humans can be useful here. Indifference prevents personal involvement in the lives of others.

The indifferent client has learned how to keep from hearing those bothersome and potentially hazardous contacts with people in need. One who is indifferent will never be taken advantage of, and one person can't solve the problems of the world anyway. People just have to learn to look after themselves. It's usually their own fault anyway. They are just lazy.

Of course, we know that this is what the Competition calls "discernment," turned onto its head. It is the indifferent person who is the lazy one, and being "wise in the ways of the world" is a great excuse for laziness. How do you think we dealt with white Christians in societies where racial minorities have been oppressed? Most whites were a little afraid of being identified as troublemakers and a lot too lazy to actually move out into the fray.

So we activated our own sleeper agents to activism, calling for liberation according to their own interpretation of the Business Plan. That made the real members of the Competition even more indifferent, since involvement identified them with our own operatives.

Oh, you can use indifference to run these mice through the most intricate mazes.

The fourth resource is the helmet of obsessive thinking. Always encourage any tendency toward obsession. Obsessive thinking does its work when the client centers on a certain thought, contemplating it endlessly to the exclusion of more significant thoughts. Again, whether the idea is true is irrelevant. The more superficial the better, but almost anything can be quite useful if it becomes overly important or such a tired cliché as to become meaningless. It starts eating away at the eardrums. The client loses perspective. To lose perspective makes clients more susceptible to the big whopper.

Obsession not only skews perspective; it generates so much background noise that the Competition's messages are hard to make out through the static.

It is one tool that sometimes catches top agents of the Competition off guard and turns their thoughts inside out. Roshtwerp was assigned to counter one of the Competition's most respected agents, a man named John Bunyan, who lived from 1628 to 1678. Bunyan damaged us through his books, but he might have caused more harm if we hadn't kept him focused on his own

worthlessness and on the notion that he must always "sell Christ
. . . sell Christ . . . sell Christ." Bunyan just couldn't get such
thoughts out of his mind, and this prevented him from engaging
in even more damaging writing.

Remember, with all the modern developments, this can be a
vital and useful tool. One of our most productive twentieth-century
salespeople was a belligerent loudmouth named Madelyn Murray
O'Hair. She went around attacking the Competition with the most
outrageous actions, until entire LCUs became obsessed with
fighting her. Every rumor about her next court case was good for
a new crusade. The woman was ridiculous, but the Competition
took her so seriously that they forgot the important things they
needed to do. We installed an entire new philosophy around them
and they didn't even notice, they were so intent on chasing their
tails to snap at a few fleas.

Another adaptation we've made using their so-called spiritual
warfare "weapons" is the "foot covering of busyness." It has become a mainstay of our defense against the Competition's sales
pitches. As human technology developed, with its laborsaving and
productivity stimulating devices, people became busier and more
distracted by minutiae. Busyness leaves them less likely to think
substantively about the Competition's marketing claims, or con-
template things of "an eternal nature."

Flambeau, this can be one of your easiest resources to use.
After all, with cell phones, pagers, the Internet, automobiles, and
airline travel, anyone—including your clients—can be kept so
harried that they have no attention left for the Competition's corporate message. That makes our job of deflecting communications easy. Just find ways to keep your clients such as Gene bogged
down in life's details. You should study the complexity and hidden distractions that we have worked into the day-to-day tasks of
managing both human life and LCUs.

Finally, when all else fails, and you need an offensive weapon, fall back on the sword of deceit. We have said some things about its use already, because in the end it is what we are all about. After all, our Infernal Founder invented the concept of lying, and our number-one corporate value is the lie and the misused truth. Deceit works in every facet of life; it is the foundation underlying our every strategic move.

Just meditate on the deceitful statement to the first human clients. "You will not surely die." I keep a flaming fountain etched with those words on my desk. Some days, especially when I look at your work, those words alone keep me from despair.

Flambeau Memorandum Seventeen

To: hotspur@darkcorp.com
From: flambeau@darkcorp.com
Subject: What about their tactics?

I have carefully examined the section of their Business Plan called Ephesians 6. Frankly, I am troubled by the confidence with which their vice president speaks of standing against our schemes and flaming arrows.

What frightens me most is this issue of "righteousness." From other reading in their corporate literature, the Romans section in particular, I gather that these creatures don't have the righteousness that the Competition CEO requires of them. It certainly follows in my experience that they are lacking in that department. Yet I also understand that the CEO's Son has found a way to give them some of his righteousness. And Paul talks here about righteousness as though it somehow turns them into steel-plated tanks.

If they figure out how to take advantage of this righteousness, I'm afraid our efforts are going to be severely hindered. I'm not altogether sure what this thing is, but it gives me the creeps. I mean Paul here seems to know a lot about our operations. He takes our powers seriously enough. But he still doesn't seem to agonize over our weapons as long as they have countermeasures such as truth and righteousness. You've said quite a lot about turning truth to our advantage. But what about righteousness?

Hotspur Memorandum Twenty-Three

To: flambeau@darkcorp.com
From: hotspur@darkcorp.com
Subject: Defensive tactical matters

In regard to your question about righteousness, I urge you to continue your careful study of the Competition's defensive armor. True, this righteousness is potentially a deadly piece of armament, simply because it doesn't come from them personally. And if they use the personal righteousness that they have been given, they can protect their hearts and emotions against our assaults of guilt. Righteousness is part of that reconciliation of which I spoke earlier. Reconciliation with the CEO depends upon their right standing before him. Otherwise, they remain at odds with him instead of with us. Notice here that Paul speaks of their "gospel of peace." They characterize their corporate message that way because the CEO's Son gives them righteousness. The righteousness allows them to be at peace with the CEO. That fact is central to their marketing strategy.

They also employ such tactics as the "assurance of salvation" (which implies assurance that they have righteousness) like a helmet to protect their minds against our arguments.

Although all of this seems quite formidable, and Paul knows that they are guaranteed success if they use this armor, we succeed because they don't use it. It is there for them, but I seldom see them wearing more than a piece or two. We make sure the pieces feel hot and restricting and generally uncomfortable.

The implications for your own strategic initiatives, Flambeau, should be obvious. When working with your clients, including Gene, hammer away with deceit. If you find your client "girded with truth," use the alternative armor I have shown you to produce despair, doubt, and confusion. You will quickly see whether a piece of their armor is weak or missing. Find the weak spot and zero in.

However, I should not need to warn you once again of the danger inherent when they read and study their corporate literature. It is their "sword of the Spirit" (Eph. 6:17 BP). I've already mentioned how the CEO's Son instantly quoted the Business Plan when our attacks came. Remember that His reference cut through the distracting challenge our CEO Below threw at Him. He sliced to the root issue, and we were badly beaten (Matt. 4:4, 7, 10 BP).

Genius that he is, our Top Guy Down Below, seized the weapon himself and creatively misused it against his chief opponent (Matt. 4:6 BP). So take note and follow the example of what our Infernal Founder did. Remember that Gene is much more susceptible to this than was their leader.

Just be glad that few of their assets are familiar with the intricacies of wielding this weapon. Fewer still employ it regularly. That's key to how we can get around the righteousness problem.

The same is true with their state-of-the-art communications equipment that they call "prayer" (Eph. 6:18 BP). According to their vice president Paul, this particular weapon is most effective when operated with intensity, alertness, perseverance, and specificity (see 6:18). I suggest you use confusion to blunt their passion, physical weariness to lower their alertness, discouragement to hinder their perseverance, and forgetfulness to keep them from specific communication. Work on disrupting it with every ounce of skill you have.

That brings me back to the statement by Paul in 2 Corinthians 10:3–4. When he refers to "weapons of our warfare," I think he has in mind the very resources he listed in Ephesians 6. Look at that segment once more and see if you can determine what it tells us about flesh and spirit.

Flambeau Memorandum Eighteen

To: hotspur@darkcorp.com
From: flambeau@darkcorp.com
Subject: Flesh and spirit

I've read some of what you posted for me on the communications channels regarding flesh and spirit, but I don't know precisely what you want me to do with it. Every demon knows that living by flesh is good and by the Holy Spirit is disastrous.

Our clients are keenly aware of the physical part of what is called the "flesh." They have weak and miserable bodies. I also know that the real "flesh" ideal is to be found in the emotional desires, and that we can help shape those desires according to what we most want.

In class, the example our teachers frequently used was the Competition's early manager of Israeli operations, David. They make over David to be some kind of hero and model. However, he was very susceptible to "the flesh," especially when he hit his midlife crisis and started looking more lustfully at beautiful members of the opposite sex. Of course, these days we can sometimes insert lust toward members of the same sex, but either way works as far as the "flesh" is concerned (2 Cor. 11:1–4 BP).

Hotspur Memorandum Twenty-Four

To: flambeau@darkcorp.com
From: hotspur@darkcorp.com
Subject: Flesh tactics

Your view of the flesh is a bit one-dimensional. Sexuality always exerts some of the most powerful fleshly pressure, but the realm of the flesh is a lot more holistic than sexual lust alone.

You need to master an understanding of how these humans work, at least as adeptly as did James, one of the Competition's first administrators. James somehow figured out the process: "Each one is tempted when he drawn away by his own desires and enticed. Then, when desire has conceived, it gives birth to sin; and sin, when it is full grown, brings forth death" (James 1:14–15 BP).

Since he followed this clear, accurate analysis of the process with the warning, "Do not be deceived" (v. 16), we figured he had some access to our business communiqués. He was related to the CEO's Son, after all.

Humans already have physical desires—for food, physical comfort, sexual satisfaction, and whatever else. We simply encourage them to find creative ways to meet those desires more fully outside the parameters fixed by the Competition. The agents assigned to David reminded him that he was in charge and could have any woman he saw. We then arranged for him to see one who fit the sexual fantasy we'd set before him. We really didn't have to do anything more. The process of desires dragging him into disaster was automatic.

So you see, while Paul may be accurate in describing the weapons available to them as "mighty in God," our strongholds generally stand firm because our competitors don't know how to employ the weapons, or else they're too careless. They are like a group of human soldiers standing guard duty who assume after several quiet nights that the enemy guerrillas have left the area. They set their weapons down, relax, watch television, read, eat or drink, become drowsy, and even doze off. When the attack comes, their superior weapons are of no value to them. Do you see what I'm getting at, Flambeau? We can more than compensate for their superior firepower. The result is that our corporate aims can be achieved, even if our total corporate assets are less powerful than theirs.

The first type of asset we have is what Paul calls a "stronghold." You may recall that in Israel the city of Jerusalem was originally a mountaintop stronghold. One of the strongest in that world was the high fortress called Masada. At Masada, a small number of Jewish humans held off a large Roman army for a long time.

We need to build such places where we can entrench evil in the lives of our clients. Any sort of evil works, from pornography to alcohol addiction or an uncontrolled temper.

Reggie, who was active in his LCU in an education and marketing post, developed a yen to find obscure truths in the Business Plan that nobody else was sharp enough to see. He thought himself "highly spiritual," an ego-rich concept that is often of use. This "intellectual stronghold" diverted his attention from chronic anger toward his spouse and a secret preoccupation with lustful pictures.

We frequently establish "strongholds" out of layers of reasoning—what Paul refers to as "arguments." These are beliefs to which the person becomes committed. They always run counter in some way to the core beliefs of our Competition's agenda.

One of our more effective "false beliefs" has to do with that "righteousness" that so concerned you in your report. Righteousness can always be subverted to the teaching that humans must perform up to a certain standard to win the full approval of their CEO's Son. This, of course, is precisely the opposite of the true working of righteousness by their CEO, his Son, and their "agent," the Holy Spirit. Humans are so easily convinced that this cannot be enough. They put more effort into their own performance and so lose out on the deep intimate relationship that their CEO wants.

Similarly, they can be persuaded that they must perform to win the approval of others. One central principle of the Competition is that what happens inside the person is of greater importance than the external appearance. But they want people to think well of them, so they try to impress others and wear masks to cover their weaknesses.

A sense of justice or fairness can be built on stones of ego to construct a fortress that wants anyone who wrongs them to feel the full force of divine and human wrath. What they may have learned about forgiveness cannot easily storm these walls.

If we can get these fortresses into their lives, they will use them as places of retreat when they realize that they have failed in some way. They fail so often that one would think they'd get used to it. But they never do. Locked away in these private strongholds they find themselves overwhelmed with shame and embarrassment and thoughts of what should have been. Shame, as you may recall, can be a deadly toxin that poisons our purposes—or it can serve us. We must know the difference and make sure shame does not lead to repentance. We always want it to lead to hopelessness.

Beyond these false reasonings, their vice president mentions "high things" or pretensions. These are the kind of arrogance-laced statements our Debased Founder proclaimed when he declared that he would become like the Most High, take over their corporate headquarters, and assume authority over the angelic divisions (Isa. 14:3–4 BP).

The classic human example of this kind of thing is a poem

written by William Ernest Henly, who became an effective agent for us as a poet. He declared himself to be the master of his fate and the captain of his soul.

However, we don't have to go to the extreme of Henly. It's enough to cause a leader to throw his weight around in an organization, insisting, "I'm in charge here." None of the Competition's corporate drivel about so-called servant leadership for this boy.

Let me share with you from my case files some additional examples of how these four specific weapons can work from our perspective. We've found that we've been able to maintain these strongholds even in the lives of some of the top agents who head up their local franchises. We often encourage and even assist them in keeping strongholds from becoming totally dominant. Instead we use them selectively to blunt the influence of these agents of the Competition.

One of your colleagues, Rachtus, was assigned to a leader in an LCU. He hadn't been able to gain any kind of edge over this individual until the man secured a new computer. Rachtus steered his first adventure on-line and pointed him to something he'd never seen before—pornography. Quickly the man was hooked. Rachtus became aware that he could easily cause this man to lose his marriage, his vocation, and the respect of others. So instead of total immersion in this "stronghold," Rachtus allowed the images to remain a secret in the man's life. Rachtus used the same strategy with the man's wife, who developed an addiction to shopping and ran up a hurtful credit card debt—not enough for bankruptcy but enough to be an ongoing distraction and worry.

You can't imagine the amount of instability Rachtus introduced into their relationship and their service to the Competition.

We've been able to introduce a great variety of false beliefs. For some, the template is, "I must perform effectively to be successful"; for another, it is, "I must be liked and accepted by others in order to succeed." We convince some: "If someone does something wrong to me or someone else, I need to make it right or get even"; or "I've failed in the past, therefore I'll always be a failure and I might as well not try anymore."

When the Competition's assets buy into this kind of erroneous logic, they're pretty effectively neutralized.

Hotspur Memorandum Twenty-Five

To: flambeau@darkcorp.com
From: hotspur@darkcorp.com
Subject: Other thought tools

We have been looking at warfare weapons and tools for a while because it is an important area. I realize that there is another entire aspect of obsession we haven't covered. You must understand the value of random, undisciplined thoughts. These can take you into fruitful territory. For example, consider the wondrous possibilities of obsessive worry.

This variation on obsessive thinking causes humans to meditate endlessly over certain concerns or worries, such as health issues, financial pressures, a potential job loss, or conflict with family members. I think in a perverse way the miserable creatures actually enjoy this kind of worrying. For one thing, they don't have to actually do anything if they feel so oppressed by the vicissitudes of life. Frequently they become distracted from any possibility of focusing on matters of substance, including taking care of their daily life responsibilities. The last thing they pay attention to is the Competition's propaganda.

We knew this would be an important area for us when we saw how much attention the CEO's Son gave to warning humans not to be anxious (Matt. 6:25–34 BP). He told them to keep their minds free of worry about sustaining a living, about keeping up with others, or about what might happen in the unknown future. If you study carefully what he had to say in that portion of the Business Plan, you'll learn just how to plant these distracting worries, Flambeau.

Keep the client focused on whether or not she'll have enough money, or whether a job layoff will happen next month, or whether his receding hairline portends health crises around the corner. Let married couples look around at other families who have more financial security, a newer automobile, or a bigger home. And don't forget to encourage a general undefined sort of insecurity about what may happen, say, a terrorist attack.

You see the point of this is not just to cause pain for the creatures. That's just a pleasant byproduct. We want to cause our clients to question the Competition's claims that the future is part of a good plan. We want to short-circuit trust. So capitalize on this strategy by planting distracting worries—thoughts that do not directly challenge the Competition's Founder but slowly erode confidence. After you've patiently nurtured worries for a time, you can question the CEO's purposes more directly, prompting the person to take the initiative instead of waiting in trust for a resolution that may never come.

I had a client who played an important role in the LCU in which she had grown up. This woman was responsible for planning both music and the training of children—not someone we want running around doing mischief. Our "in" with this client was that she worried about her past. She had been a victim of abuse, and she let it become her deep, dark secret.

An uncle had abused her many years before, but her mind had tried to suppress most of the details. She didn't know exactly how or why, but she had been corrupted by "something." I kept pointing out similarities between the vague picture she had of her uncle and her father. Eventually she decided that "it must have been my dad." I began superimposing his picture on those vague memories, using our "sharpening technique" to bring those false memories into focus as though they were true pictures of what had happened.

Eventually I convinced her that her father had been guilty, and she must confront him with what she now remembered that he had done. The result was a most delightfully bitter scene of retribution in front of the family. The father could only deny her accusations, which made him more despicable in her sight.

She began spreading her "memories" around, so that all would know the truth about this "evil man." The LCU was polarized by her accusations, some siding with her and others supporting her parents. She went to the leaders, insisting that they "throw him out." They countered that there was no proof of her allegations, to which she responded that her memories were all the truth they should require. I was delighted when she and her husband left the LCU, took their children, and moved to another city, vowing never to allow any contact between her children and the grandparents. The LCU was left in ruins. The managers had to ignore the Competition's Business Plan and spend all their time putting out fires from this conflict.

Flambeau Memorandum Nineteen

To: hotspur@darkcorp.com
From: flambeau@darkcorp.com
Subject: Spiritual alternatives

Much of our work in the thoughts of our clients has been designed to make them morally vulnerable or prone to despair when things go wrong. But you haven't said much about getting them involved in false faiths—the old idol worship gambit. I know of some tempters that have had good success getting clients into spiritual alternatives, especially using the Internet. What a lush marketplace of spirituality it can be.

It would seem that this is one of our great opportunities just now, the Internet and the plethora of our own belief systems that have thrived under the New Age-Postmodern era.

Gene works with a woman who is involved in one of our transplanted Eastern religious cults. I've tried to get him to see her attractive qualities and deep spirituality. So far he just thinks her a little too weird. He has talked to her about his beliefs, but she isn't very adept at presenting hers to him. What is your perspective on this aspect of the flesh-spirit battlefield?

Hotspur Memorandum Twenty-Six

To: flambeau@darkcorp.com
From: hotspur@darkcorp.com
Subject: Alternative therapy

I tend to lump the kinds of things you mention under the tool of *pretension*. A pretension is any system of thought that dilutes or distorts the Competition's agenda in the name of personal fulfillment. The pretension is that the individual thinks he or she can discover truth within. Then we can always add that "truth" only means the way of life that works for "me." My truth is not necessarily your truth, and you certainly wouldn't dare to impose your ideas onto my belief system. Obviously the Internet is ideal for this sort of nonsense. For the price of a domain name, anyone's belief system can be thrown into the mix to draw disciples, along with all the other belief systems.

And the Internet is a medium of self-discovery. The "surfer" can wander into some chat room and suddenly have an epiphany that this must be the virtual truth, which has been uncovered at last by the Pentium II processor and intrepid mouse. You'd think some of these folks had discovered life on Saturn for all their excitement.

In the society in which you are working, one of the classic examples of an alternative belief system came along in the 1860s. I'm speaking of the philosophy of materialist evolution, or macroevolution, which gave a possible belief option for creation without a creator. It rapidly became one of our more effective marketing packages and remains so today, regardless of its lack of credibility as a theory.

You mention the New Age complex of beliefs, which actually is older than evolutionary thought, dating in one form or another back to the 1600s. But New Age gained an exciting new lease on life when Oriental religions began drifting back into fashion in Europe and North America in the 1950s.

New Age thought is incredibly effective because it takes in so many kinds of ideas. It is a pick-and-choose smorgasbord. The key element, though, has been the idea that each person has a spiritual journey, and none of the paths can be called wrong. We have done well in infiltrating this idea into the local competition units. Our core message in this initiative has been that the only bad truth is an exclusive absolute truth.

Under the vague umbrella of the New Age movement stand all sorts of exciting syncretistic religions. Some of the best merge the Competition's corporate agenda with ours. We've even had some small success marketing our own house religion, Wicca, as a nature-environmentalist way to honor the physical world. Marketing has come up with some unique packaging that even reaches into children's educational systems.

Some time ago, Veldrake, a contemporary of yours, was assigned to work with a teacher in one of their "Christian school" organizations—a thinly disguised Competition marketing outpost. These organizations historically pride themselves on maintaining "purity of doctrine" in what they teach. However, Veldrake's client was persuaded to attend a seminar on new forms of spiritual education that open up the children to the "divinity within." This teacher represented us among her students for years until the board realized what she was really teaching and asked her to leave.

Strategic Initiative Five:
Mixing Truth and Lies

Oh, that you would bear with me in a little folly—and indeed you do bear with me. For I am jealous for you

with godly jealousy. For I have betrothed you to one husband, that I may present you as a chaste virgin to Christ.

But I fear, lest somehow, as the serpent deceived Eve
by his craftiness, so your minds may be corrupted from
the simplicity that is in Christ. For if he who comes
preaches another Jesus whom we have not preached, or
if you receive a different spirit which you have not received, or a different gospel which you have not accepted,
you may well put up with it. . . .

But what I do, I will also continue to do, that I may cut
off the opportunity from those who desire an opportunity
to be regarded just as we are in the things of which they
boast. For such are false apostles, deceitful workers, trans-
forming themselves into apostles of Christ.

And no wonder! For Satan himself transforms himself
into an angel of light. Therefore it is no great thing if his
ministers also transform themselves into ministers of righteousness, whose end will be according to their works.
(2 Cor. 11:1–4, 12–15 BP)

Flambeau Memorandum Twenty

To: hotspur@darkcorp.com
From: flambeau@darkcorp.com
Subject: Deceptive distortion

It appears that one of the best ways to implant our corporate message into the Competition's minions is through our Infernal Founder's strategy of distortion.

Questions came to mind as I perused the portion of their Business Plan the Competition refers to as 2 Corinthians 11:1–15. There's a great deal here about our CEO Below's incredible skill in craftiness or trickery. This seemed to be a key concept around which their vice president wrapped a lot of his discussion of our strategy. The word that Paul used to refer to our "craftiness" literally means "ready to do anything." The Top Guy Down Below has frequently presented it as the lowest or the ultimate of virtues.

Since craftiness is so important to our strategy, I decided to see where else the idea turns up in their corporate literature. For example, when their CEO's Son was questioned by our Herodian agents, they raised the double-edged question, "Is it lawful for us to pay taxes to Caesar or not?" (Luke 20:22 BP). Now that was crafty.

A similar word turns up in their earlier corporate history, when our Debased Leader dumped a fearsome set of trials on their agent Job. His "friend" Eliphaz threw at Job their proverb, "He catches the wise in their own craftiness, and the counsel of the cunning comes quickly upon them" (Job 5:13 BP). Paul used the same proverb in 1 Corinthians 3:19. I suppose his point was that no one could be more cunning and crafty than their CEO.

Second, I wonder why Paul set such emphasis on history. I

know our Founder was able to carry out a successful takeover operation at the start of our Eden Operations. It's great to go back and celebrate the way our Enterprising Founder duped the wife of their first Earth Division head and dragged the first human pair down into the primal slime. While it was one of our finest corporate hours, I'm not sure why the Competition's vice president would include it in their corporate literature now. It certainly wasn't one of their high points.

There's a third observation I draw from this portion of their documents. We apparently did succeed in getting their vice president to adopt some of our strategic marketing initiatives. After all, he admits to jealousy—something both you and Scraptus emphasized. I know boasting to be one of the major traits exhibited by our Infernal Founder. Consequently, for their VP to admit to boasting, I would say, constitutes a major coup. Perhaps that should make our acquisition targets much easier to achieve.

I must admit, I don't get the betrothal or marriage allusion. This is another example of a compulsion to drag out some historical relic custom just to prove a point.

The most important fact in this whole section is that their VP concedes that our marketing efforts are diluting his attempts to get their corporate message out. I've seen the same kind of strategies employed in some of these humans' pitiful secular marketing initiatives. For example, a local bank is taken over by a national corporation. Immediately, all the other banks focus public attention on the benefits of being locally owned. Never mind that what they're saying has very little relationship to reality. Both use local people and the same money management programs. But the local ownership establishes an emotional connection.

The same thing happens with the marketing of their beverages. The other day I was looking over the shoulder of my client Gene as he flew home from a business trip. The magazine he was reading showed one of the large beer companies repositioning itself as hip, young, and attractive, implying that the Competition had become stodgy and out-of-date.

I couldn't help noting their VP's emphasis on our people. Apparently, our representatives in the local competition unit in Corinth were skilled at employing the tricky tactics of our Founder. It was clear from Paul's reference to them as "super apostles"— apparently a spin-off on their archaic leadership structure and the term they used for some of their early vice presidents—that he felt that our reps were highly credible and that their message was at least being tolerated. I'm not sure how they managed to achieve this. Perhaps you'll have some thoughts as to how they did it, and how I can capitalize on their successful strategies.

As I understand it, the concept of *apostle* has to do with those who held a position of upper management. It seems to be used almost interchangeably with the term *disciple* (for example, in Matthew 10:2 of their Business Plan). It seems evident, due to the nature of this word, that it looks more at their corporate function, since it means to be "sent forth." *Disciple* refers to some corporate relationship with the CEO's Son.

One last observation is that their VP Paul made a big deal over the fact that he had a right to carry this title of "apostle." In his first memo to Corinth, he raised the question, "Am I not an apostle?" as though this were a disputed matter (1 Cor. 9:1 BP). Now he again goes into some detail about how the so-called "signs of the apostle" were accomplished within the Corinthian LCU, apparently during his tenure there.

I think I'm beginning to get the hang of this, Hotspur. I know I've overlooked a couple of things in some of my earlier letters. I think I'm missing less now, and probably doing a better job as a result.

Hotspur Memorandum Twenty-Seven

To: flambeau@darkcorp.com
From: hotspur@darkcorp.com
Subject: Your distortions

Flaming tarantulas! What good thing did I do to deserve such a dim coal of brimstone?

You missed all the concepts I hoped you would find in 1 Corinthians 11 of the Business Plan and got everything else all wrong. Your assessment of your own meager efforts—suggesting that you were missing less and becoming more effective—would get you into trouble if it wasn't distorted and deceitful. That's the only good thing I can say about your most recent communication.

To begin with, let me deal with some of your sloppy demonic musings. You are making the kinds of stupid mistakes in understanding their corporate literature that we try to get them to make. Then I'll try to bring you up to speed on one of the vital components of our corporate mission.

Jealousy and boasting are fine and good. But there are two kinds of jealousy and two kinds of boasting from the perspective of the Competition's corporate literature. The object makes the difference. Do the jealousy and boasting aim at the uplifting of self or the uplifting of other people and the CEO? We want the first kind, but never the second.

A lover expresses a kind of selfish jealousy when he wants his lover to focus all of her affection and attention on him. And there is a kind of jealousy a father feels for his daughter's purity as he prepares to present her in marriage. The father's jealousy is for the honor of the daughter and her future marriage. I know you have very little frame of reference for this kind of thing, since it's one of our Competition's corporate values. But you need to understand that this is what their vice president was talking about.

It's the same with boasting. Sure, one of our major values is to boast over personal achievement, recognition, success, and even material things. However, their VP was using a gentle cousin to sarcasm called irony in order to make his point. He was using his boasting to show the difference between the work of our agents and his efforts.

If you had more carefully examined this portion of their corporate literature, you would have discovered three reasons for his boasting and jealousy that do us no good at all: First, he saw their vulnerability to our attacks (1 Cor. 11:2–3 BP). Second, he saw their receptivity to our message (11:4). Third, he feared that they would not listen to his warnings about us because we were feeding them the line that he was not a *real* apostle (11:5).

You were inadequate in your observations concerning the words disciple and apostle as well. Had you not been such a pea brain, you would not have missed an important distinction in this term *apostle*, over which you raised such a big question. All you needed to do was make the same sort of word study that you did with *craftiness*, looking at all uses in the Business Plan.

Their CEO's Son surrounded Himself with lots of *disciples*, then established an inner circle from among them to train as *apostles*. Surely you know that the point of the LCU is to make disciples. Haven't you figured out that fruitful discipleship and worship are their main products? Apostles were given special authority as vice presidents to represent the CEO's Son in establishing His work. But once that work was established, the representation passed to the corporate body and all of its franchises. That's why there are no more individual "apostles," though some people are still "sent out" by the Competition to be sales reps around the world. All of them together carry out the work that the first vice presidents organized.

Although honor was attached to the *apostle* designation in the first business units, it was not a pleasant or profitable position. Paul said that he and the other apostles were condemned to a life characterized by humiliation and death before the world (1 Cor. 4:9 BP).

Even though holding this title could have been an occasion for self-building pride, it also forced one to constantly measure himself in terms of the CEO's Son represented. Paul especially felt that he was "the least of the apostles" (1 Cor. 15:8–9 BP). In 2 Corinthians 11 he warned that, least or not, they had better listen to him or we would pick them off.

And, of course, he was exactly correct.

Hotspur Memorandum Twenty-Eight

To: flambeau@darkcorp.com
From: hotspur@darkcorp.com
Subject: Stealth strategy and marketing savvy

I've had time to calm down and reflect more on your last report. I'm trying to detect anything usable in it. While it isn't exactly a grand insight, I'll concede that you did pick up on their vice president's reference to our greatest corporate success. Do I detect a whiff of downgrading the importance of that success because it has become old news? I hope I don't have to remind you that we are in business today because of that great event, and our CEO Below doesn't like us to forget it. Keep that in mind, or you could find yourself toasted by the Top Guy himself.

As to why their corporate vice president would call attention to this event, use your pointed head, demon! He's suggesting that Corinth could become another Eden disaster if they don't shape up. The analogy should be clear; their local franchise stood in a similar position to that of the first human family when we deceived them. The Competition likes to remind their people to resist our efforts and agents (see, for example, James 4:7 and 1 Peter 5:9 of their Business Plan).

Paul feared that these Corinthians were being completely duped, to the point that they would leave the simplicity of the corporate message built around the Son of their Founder (1 Cor. 11:3 BP).

I call this mode of deception our "stealth strategy." You should have picked up on the fact that they used terms that can be translated "masquerade" or "transform" no less than three times in 11:13–15. Remember the big deal when humans figured out how to build an aircraft that didn't show up on radar? It's the same with our corporate technology. It is our mission to disguise ourselves as bona fide representatives of the Competition. Remember the inscription over the door of corporate headquarters: "Our first corporate value is deception." Let that sink between your pointed ears and become at home in that infinitesimal mind. We achieve successes by good stealth marketing.

We have devised numerous stealth marketing strategies, all of them mentioned somewhere in their corporate literature. We have a message that runs totally counter to theirs. Our job is to make sure it doesn't seem so different, that the contrast appears in shades of gray.

That's where your skill at deception comes into play.

The marriage illustration applies here. Their Israeli division was actually viewed as the "bride of God" in Isaiah 54:5 and 62:5. At Jewish weddings, two friends of the bridegroom carried out many duties, one of which was to ceremonially certify the chastity of the bride. Vice president Paul was putting himself in the place of this "friend of the bridegroom." The Corinthian's business unit had been betrothed to the CEO's Son, and Paul wanted to certify that they were chaste. He was expressing his desire to see them finish up their time on earth by maintaining their purity of commitment to the Competition.

This brings us back to the fact that our job is to keep LCUs seduced the way our Boss conned the first woman. Remember how he did it? He caused her to question their CEO's corporate mandate about eating of all the trees of Eden except one. He led her to distort her CEO's instructions and to question His motive and integrity. The stealth idea he introduced was that she and her miserable spouse could actually have as much authority as their CEO (Gen. 3:1–5 BP).

Our clients need to know the attractiveness of our message and the limits of what the Competition offers. They especially need to hear our "be your own CEO" pitch again and again. Spiritual

entrepreneurialism, Flambeau, that's the great stealth message—
the essence of our corporate objectives. We want to create a client
base of spiritual entrepreneurs from among those who've given
allegiance to the Competition. That's really what our corporate
raiding efforts are all about. To succeed, we must probe and test
to see which of their personnel qualifies as a takeover target and
which is out of our ultimate reach but can be neutralized.

Let me talk a bit about corporate branding in this stealth marketing campaign. Human corporations want people to think of
their brand name first in relation to a product. The ideal is for a
specific brand to become the reference point for the product. Many
years ago, small soft drink bottling companies were organized in
every small and large city of North America. One of them, Coca-
Cola, began investing enormous resources into advertising to make
certain that people began to think of soft drinks as "Cokes." Much
more recently, the marketers of Pepsi Cola worked very hard to
break Coca-Cola's hold on market identification for specific age
groups. This battle goes on for most human products and services. Seldom are there significant differences. Perception of su-
premacy is the reality.

We are at a slight disadvantage in that our product is not something that humans want once they find out too much about it. This
is why stealth deception—evading radar—is crucial. These days
our marketing brands us as the pacesetters in spirituality. This
can sound plausible to even the narrowest thinking officer of the
Competition's corporate structure. But it's broad enough to include all our far-flung corporate divisions—from major religions
and minor cults to the occult and "non-religion" spiritual values.
Remember that each of these spiritualities has its unique "values." It's fine to have humans defend their values. It distracts them
from serious consideration of what the Competition identifies as
virtues. Of course, it is not a good idea for them to know that our

corporate values are lying, trickery, intimidation, and manipulation. They might get the idea that they can't trust us!

Part of marketing is to identify code words that give the right impression. A lot of research has been directed at picking these words, and they change somewhat from generation to generation. Some of our best words to use now are *broad*, *inclusive*, and *tolerant*. These can be passed off as corporate values, though they are not really values at all. Broad thinking is an attitude toward values, not a value in itself. You might call it an "anti-value" value. The inclusivist basically believes that everyone should be included in the good things offered by their CEO. Beliefs and values have no part in determining membership.

Marketing also works to undermine opposition by attaching negative connotations to words they use to describe themselves. Our marketing research and development has done some of its best work in this area. Such concepts as *doctrinal understanding* and *absolute truth* stir real animosity today. I'm sure you've heard the expression that the Competition is not "a religion" but "a relationship." What logical mush to think that a human can have the one without the other. But they fall for it and are vulnerable to the notion that the important thing is a subjective feeling of intimacy, not the daily reality of living a life of connection to their CEO.

We developed this word redefinition marketing strategy. One of our first maneuvers, one that still works well, is to change the meaning of their corporate message—what they usually call the "gospel." Technically the word means "good news," and they use it to define what the CEO's Son did so that they can have life (see 1 Cor. 15:3–4 BP). That is such a narrow understanding. We can always improve upon it just a touch by adding a little something to the meaning. Paul just about went into screaming fits when we pulled this in the Galatian LCUs (see Gal. 1:6–7 BP). He said we had "perverted the gospel." Imagine that.

In Galatia and some of the other early LCUs, we actually made the meaning of *gospel* more restrictive. These days we usually go in the other direction: It's fine to "believe" so long as one doesn't go "fundamentalist" about it, since "all roads lead to where you want to go, and you can be like the CEO and chose your own way."

Incidentally, have you noticed our coup in redefining *fundamentalist*? This word originally was a technical designation referring to "The Fundamentals," a series of books that promoted a narrowly defined conservative viewpoint. First we implied that "fundies" were radical bigots who didn't believe in "proven" truths such as evolution. They were obscurantists and none too intelligent, like the folks who handle rattlesnakes in their LCU meetings. Then we expanded the term to cover all serious members of the Competition, whatever their views on the original distinctives of the group. Finally we added in all the far-out fringe groups in other world religions, so that there are fundamentalist Muslims and Hindus who go around killing people in the name of their faith, and fundamentalists in the Competition's camp who are liable to be found bombing abortion clinics. Now they are all considered strange and dangerous.

I tell you, Flambeau—marketing is a beautiful thing.

Flambeau Memorandum Twenty-One

To: hotspur@darkcorp.com
From: flambeau@darkcorp.com
Subject: Deceptive distortion and your stealth idea

If I am not "missing the point" in your estimation once more, you seem to be saying that what you call "stealth marketing" is nothing more than identifying the different sorts of people we want to reach and telling each what they want to hear. If so, why don't you just say so, instead of making it sound like it requires post-doctoral study in temptation engineering. I'm sure we have done some spectacular work in this regard, but let's not overstate the matter.

I find it frustrating that we never know for sure whether a client has gone to the other company so fully that he or she is under the CEO's permanent protection. So I don't know whether to try to recapture clients or to focus my efforts on neutralizing their influence. I'd like to think that I might reacquire Gene, since he hasn't been under their influence too long. I know some cross that line quickly, while others hover just on our side of it, ready to jump over if things look better with them than with us. Our work on the concept that a human can choose to make the CEO's Son "Savior" but not "Lord" until some later time, if ever, has been a fairly useful tool. These border-dwelling humans think they can live on the side of the line that "punches their ticket" and never bother to read the fine print about the true significance of "producing fruit" for the Competition.

But as far as I can tell, Gene doesn't live in this delusional middle ground. He wants to wear the leg irons and wedding ring. On the other hand, he has a hard time actually living out this "discipleship," which gives me hope that he hasn't arrived yet. Or at least I can use his weaknesses to turn off others who are looking to see if the CEO's Son—and folks at the Glencrest franchise—are real.

I suppose the same basic strategies work either to get him back or to neutralize his effects if we cannot reacquire him permanently as ours.

Gene has progressed beyond the first blush of enthusiasm for all things pertaining to the CEO's Son. He has gotten to know people of Glencrest well enough to see their flaws. They have disappointed Him on more than one occasion. So he may be starting to think that allegiance to their corporation is not all it's cracked up to be. That may allow me to capitalize on his disillusionment and pressure him back in our direction. I think their clients are most vulnerable when the so-called honeymoon phase of their allegiance has just passed.

I'm sure you'll have more to say about marketing to these recent defections.

Hotspur Memorandum Twenty-Nine

To: flambeau@darkcorp.com
From: hotspur@darkcorp.com
Subject: Countering loyalty to the CEO's Son

Look carefully at the 2 Corinthians 11 portion of their Business Plan. You will see components of their corporate message that must be countered if you are to have much marketing success with Gene and other newcomers at the other company. It bothers me that you more inexperienced demons first let these clients slip through your fingers and then seem ready to move hell and earth to get them back.

So long as the CEO's Son hasn't become a living reality in people's lives, it still is possible to redefine him any way we wish. Go back and look carefully at 11:4. Here's the key to our corporate message—another Jesus. They can accept this Jesus as a good man, a corporate leader, even a martyr to a cause. He was a victim who was hammered in a corporate shakeup by others on their way to the top. Whatever.

The only thing is that they can't accept Him as the perfect incarnation of their Founder. Nor can they trust His death as payment for their failures. That part of their message simply must be confounded.

You refer to the lordship scheme. This is an aspect of what we have been calling "mind-blinding." It works quite effectively on those who want security without the lifestyle of discipleship. But you shouldn't put too much security in it either. It has two basic weaknesses.

First, a lot of the humans who defect from our side are wired toward oversensitivity about their faults. Some are so hung up over feelings of unworthiness that they may refuse to accept the label of disciple. That neutralizes the efforts they might have made, which is good. It does not, however, mean that their CEO hasn't accepted them. There are people who have trouble accepting acceptance. Ironically, they actually have a more accurate self-image than do others; their difficulty is in understanding the depth of what the Competition calls mercy. But the bottom line is that they love Him and He loves them and that's the end of our reacquisition efforts. Since we can't really see them through His Son's eyes (which must be a truly disgusting view), we can waste a lot of effort by taking the wrong approach.

Second, the Competition does not like to allow the status quo to continue indefinitely with "fringers." I have seen a sideline person crumple to our temptation, only to realize that this failure was just what their CEO's Spirit had been waiting for. Frequently it isn't until they swoop in to acquire that we find out we've been had.

If you can keep them thinking that they enjoy all the Competition's benefits without this troublesome "lordship" business, and if you can involve them in the LCUs, they make strong sleeper agents—real saboteurs if used correctly. Sometimes they reach management level positions and become important assets for our cause.

Now, I appreciate the uncertainty about knowing where a client really is. I've experienced a great deal of it myself. You should make an educated guess, though. Do not think that the same tempter principles apply whether you are silencing a noisy member of the Competition, bringing a wandering soul back to our ministrations, or maintaining a client in a mental twilight.

When in doubt, remember that the Competition's focus is always on the person of the CEO's Son. Individually or corporately, our emphasis must be on countering that exclusive loyalty to Him.

Flambeau Memorandum Twenty-Two

To: hotspur@darkcorp.com
From: flambeau@darkcorp.com
Subject: Beating loyalty

I'm wondering about the best countermeasures to loyalty. An example of one shiny new possibility comes to mind since agents from our radical Arab corporate structure attacked certain national and international symbols with great loss of life. Since then it has been considered good to accord extra understanding toward Islamic franchises. My impression is that our planners only anticipated starting an old-fashioned global war. Their maneuvers took us in that direction at least.

What I never would have expected, and I wonder if they did, was the serendipity that many who are attached to the Competition's franchises began tying themselves into knots to accept members of another religion as fellows in faith. It's suddenly become popular to proclaim that they are all just one peace-loving community of fellow travelers down the road of faith. Anyone who speaks loudly about exclusive loyalty to the CEO's Son is, ergo, a bigot. This seems to fit wonderfully into our agenda of portraying the CEO's Son as only one of many good, worthy, and acceptable corporate pioneers, any of whom can be followed.

I guess there are all sorts of these possibilities in the politically correct world of humans. The trouble is, some go so far that you certainly wouldn't call them "subtle" would you? I suspect that not everyone is going to buy this packaging.

Hotspur Memorandum Thirty

To: flambeau@darkcorp.com
From: hotspur@darkcorp.com
Subject: Countering loyalty to the CEO's Son

Yes, there are a number of ways that human society is taking care of the loyalty issue for us, almost automatically. You mention one contribution of our strategists. These demons are experts at manipulation on a global scale. I doubt you will want them to hear your comment that this recent success was something they just "fell into." They have been playing racial and religious wars for centuries and know how to nuance all of the factors. Meanwhile, why don't you worry less about global cultural policy and more about Gene and your other specific clients? You are right that not all of them will buy into our little brotherhood campaign.

Remember: Exclusivity and loyalty to their CEO's Son poses one of the greatest threats to our corporate agenda. It simply must stop, whether or not you have flubbed your assignment with Gene irreparably, as I believe you have.

I would suggest you gain a better understanding of the other stealth maneuvers that are mentioned in 2 Corinthians 4:11. We could say much more about the first, introducing "a different Jesus" into the LCU frame of reference. Another element their vice president mentions is "a different spirit."

They make so much of the presence that the CEO puts into their hearts, a corporate power source they call the "Holy Spirit." It's fine to allow them to think of this as a vague impersonal influence or a psychological attitude. It is best that they not be allowed to think of this inner presence as a Person of the CEO who proceeds from the Founder and His Son.

Remember, our key to success is deception through diversion. We cannot comprehend how their CEO puts this Presence in them. Certainly none of us can understand why He would dirty himself in the little cesspools they call their minds.

Fortunately, they also have an incomplete understanding, so they tend to creatively fill in the details and spend a lot of time focusing on this Presence. That actually is good for us. Their CEO intends for this "Spirit" to focus interest upon Him and His Son, while he initiates countermeasures through the personal Presence to thwart us.

Sometimes the best thing we can do to keep some tool of the Competition in check is to make its use an absolute obsession. If we can stir endless debate on arguments about the Presence, the CEO's power will be underused, and the focus will be skewed. That, Flambeau, is stealth marketing at its best.

We also can deal with their loyalty by diluting their core message to make it seem less vital. Note the phrase "a different gospel." We don't mind them presenting a message of self-esteem, racial and ethnic tolerance, passion for the poor, or personal good works as a way to earn corporate favor. What we have to do is make that cross as nasty and offensive as possible (see 1 Cor. 1:23–30 BP). We have to blunt the focus of their message that their Founder's Son in some way paid for their actions. They must not know His full loyalty to them while they followed our CEO.

Power is released when they set their loyalty in the CEO's Son because they have fully grasped the significance of what happened during His incursion into human form. Once the Presence in them attaches the Son's loyalty to their loyalty, a chemical bond takes hold that not even the Top Guy Down Below can break. If you can't deal with the loyalty issue before it reaches this "faith alone" stage, you can kiss their souls good-bye.

Flambeau Memorandum Twenty-Three

To: hotspur@darkcorp.com
From: flambeau@darkcorp.com
Subject: Money motivation

I noticed at this point in the Competition's corporate literature (2 Cor. 11:7–9), Paul returns to the issue of money paid for his own ministry. He puts quite an emphasis on money in other places, but here he seems sensitive to the charge that he is a drain on their bottom line.

Money always is a formidable weapon, but I'm not sure what instruction I should take from this point. As I read this, I gathered that their vice president seemed to have put up with a lot of grief from the likes of these saps, not to mention all sorts of other difficulties in his life, without an ongoing salary or benefits package. He received no stock options, no bonuses, no medical insurance or 401K.

I do recall that he took some money for personal expenses from the franchise in Philippi (Phil. 4:10, 15–16 BP). So why was he so insistent about not taking anything at Corinth? Certainly none of them could have said that he didn't deserve it, and the city was not exactly destitute.

Apparently our agents in the Corinthian LCU didn't hesitate to take money when they could. The fact that their teaching came with a monetary price tag gave it greater perceived value than Paul's among the "bottom line" folks. So our teachers won more esteem because they took the money. At least, that's the impression I have from the literature. People appreciate what they pay for.

Hotspur Memorandum Thirty-One

To: flambeau@darkcorp.com
From: hotspur@darkcorp.com
Subject: Stealth personnel

In your latest communication, you are too dense to realize that your last paragraph answers the question you were asking about money.

We cannot get across our corporate message without the right corporate personnel. This is why we emphasize infiltrating their LCUs with our own corporate agents. It's also why corporate take-over remains a keystone strategy. If we can turn a Glencrest into our own franchise by filling key positions with our solid agents, we can make the LCU a trap for wandering clients and a force to undermine the Competition's higher corporate structure as well. Time and again this strategy has wiped out whole centers of their CEO's authority, replacing them with a phantom business structure that serves us.

Paul saw this happening in the Corinth LCUs, and he sought to counter it with a way to discern our people from theirs. The difference was that ours were mostly interested in getting ahead financially, while theirs were interested in serving their CEO and the people. You should have been able to discern that Paul was being radical about not taking their money because he was making a point of showing the difference between their agents and ours.

We infiltrated Corinth with a crew who gained a reputation as "super apostles." These were servants of our CEO, who had "transformed themselves" (2 Cor. 11:15 BP).

In conjunction with our stealth technology, we had these "super apostles" insist that their version of the Competition's corporate message was superior to Paul's. The Corinthians listened to and actually welcomed their message. That Paul labeled them "superlative" representatives underscores how effectively they had demonstrated the virtue of conceit.

Why don't you try this, Flambeau? Draft some clients who show a lot of innate arrogance, cultivate conceit, mix it with intellectual pride, and send them in to show why our message is better than their tired old one. For this you need to find outstanding communicators. Historically, successful radio and television communicators have filled the bill nicely. That genre doesn't have as much influence today, though, so look locally for dynamic personalities to recruit.

The people we employed in Corinth were exceptionally skilled in speaking; they sounded intellectual, erudite, and convincing. In fact, by his own admission, Paul was nowhere near as skilled (see 2 Cor. 11:6 BP).

The best way to secure such people is through financial motivation. As you should know, one of our core values is materialism, what the Competition refers to as "the lust of the eyes" (1 John 2:13 BP), or the "love of money," which they acknowledge to be the root of all kinds of evil. You should learn from the operation of human corporations, Flambeau, just how effective this can be. Influence buying, corporate slush funds, padded expense accounts—these are powerful tools. Our agents didn't hesitate to multiply their own personal assets through their careers as they diffused the light from the Competition's corporate message.

A question frequently comes up at this point: How do we put together an attractive financial package from an LCU budget? Obviously the mega-LCUs are easier pickings if you are working the profit motive. Big media units are the easiest, but there are fewer of them these days, and we've been using greed to attract people to them so long that the profits have fallen off. Other large groups often have very careful lay boards of deeply committed business people. They are used to spotting profiteers and can be hard to maneuver.

For units the size of Glencrest, ambition is probably the best profit motivator. If there is a sufficient take now, an ambitious leader will snap it up while aiming for a sweeter "pie by and by." Stepping stone leaders are excellent. They want to make a name, they usually are charismatic, and they have a minimum of pretensions about actually caring for the LCU gathered in front of them.

Future gain isn't your only recruiting incentive, though. Some people are hungrier for less material gain if they can have sufficient material authority. This "kingdom-building instinct" is strong in humans. It can produce the best materialism. Clients will do anything and say anything to be the CEO—which means that the real CEO and the CEO's Son lose their executive parking spots. Even outside the top management spots, people can be recruited by the desire for power, and you won't have to find a dime of remuneration for them. They will gladly sell their souls to you just to have a say in the building program or the search committee. This sort of materialist comes cheap.

Again, you should be able to see that this is the reason why Paul made a major issue out of the fact that he did not profit financially from his services. They know, as we do, how easily these humans are swayed by material gain. After all, financial corruption can be just as effective as moral or doctrinal corruption. We don't care which direction they move, as long as we get the Competition's agents off track.

Strategic Initiative Six:
Intimidation

It is doubtless not profitable for me to boast. I will come to visions and revelations of the Lord: I know a man in Christ who fourteen years ago—whether in the body I do not know, or whether out of the body I do not know, God knows—such a one was caught up to the third heaven. And I know of such a man—whether in the body or out of the body I do not know, God knows—how he was caught up into Paradise and heard inexpressible words, which it is not lawful for a man to utter. Of such a one I will boast; yet of myself I will not boast, except in my infirmities.

For though I might desire to boast, I will not be a fool; for I will speak the truth. But I refrain, lest anyone should think of me above what he sees me to be or hears from me.

And lest I should be exalted above measure by the abundance of the revelations, a thorn in the flesh was given to me, a messenger of Satan to buffet me, lest I be exalted above measure. Concerning this thing I pleaded with the Lord three times that it might depart from me. And He said to me, "My grace is sufficient for you, for My strength is made perfect in weakness."

Therefore most gladly I will rather boast in my infirmities, that the power of Christ may rest upon me. Therefore I take pleasure in infirmities, in reproaches, in needs, in persecutions, in distresses, for Christ's sake. For when I am weak, then I am strong. (2 Cor. 12:1–10 BP)

Flambeau Memorandum Twenty-Four

To: hotspur@darkcorp.com
From: flambeau@darkcorp.com
Subject: Thorny thorn-in-the-flesh questions

I referred back to our first correspondence to see the progression of subjects their vice president covered in the 2 Corinthians Business Plan. Our set of strategies runs something like this:

1. Cultivate conflict.
2. Mind-blind.
3. Arrange joint ventures.
4. Wage war for the mind.
5. Confuse with our lies their main truth.

Now I have reached the one about which I have the most questions—*Intimidate and discourage with painful life experiences.* This is found in 2 Corinthians 12:7.

It seems to me that the major thing we need to note about the Competition's understanding of our strategy is that *our CEO* sent a message of pain to *their* vice president. Paul was pretty explicit that our Big Guy was the source. When I first examined this section, I assumed that the "thorn in the flesh" was one of our forms of intimidation. Scraptus said something about pain intimidation as foundational tempting—one of our most basic tools.

So why does the vice president make such a point of this as a positive experience, one that he can boast about? He almost sounds arrogant about it, as if it is something that was given to him as a blessing. No, I'm not going to bring up "boasting" again. You've already doused my ideas on that with boiling oil.

Obviously the story told in 2 Corinthians 12:1–4 about a man who visited their corporate headquarters referred to Paul himself, but on the whole it presents a curiously cryptic message. There seems to be a dynamic interaction between their CEO and ours in Paul's life in a confrontation that ultimately served their cause, not ours. Quite frankly, it seems our intimidation by a thorn in the flesh was a total wash-out.

I can't help but think about the young woman Joni Eareckson Tada, for whom we arranged a swimming accident that broke her neck. She had been barely interested in the Competition and at worst would have ended up in a cozy wife and mother role, with LCU meetings once or twice a week.

Paralyzed, she became one of the Competition's most vocal agent provocateurs, working tirelessly to foster the values we hate.

This brings up some rather disturbing possibilities about our use of intimidation. Sometimes this tiger forgets which direction it is supposed to attack, and we end up mauled instead of the intended victim.

Hotspur Memorandum Thirty-Two

To: flambeau@darkcorp.com
From: hotspur@darkcorp.com
Subject: Intimidation through the "Job's Wife Factor"

What you are referring to is the "Job Factor," or perhaps we should be more current and refer to it as the "Joni Factor," if you like. Obviously we don't know how intimidation will turn out once their CEO gets hold of it. And yes, it is used by the Competition's CEO. It was our efforts that turned Job into the heroic figure he became in the Competition's Business Plan. We have been bitten badly by inflicted pain and suffering in the lives of many Pauls and Jonis.

Does it then follow that we shouldn't do it? Hardly. Pain and suffering are not the real tools that get us what we want. *Fear* of pain and suffering and *bitterness* caused by pain and suffering are the real tools. They are powerful.

For every Job there is a Job's wife, who is shoved into bitterness and despair and disillusionment by the effects of our work. It is for her that we continue to ply this technique, not for the Jobs who, in the words of the old watch commercials, "take a lickin' and keep on tickin'."

Our Enterprising Founder loves to use manipulation, misdirection, disguise, and deception. But those tools often don't work either. As I said before, there are no guarantees in this business. When things aren't going well, sometimes taking off the gloves and placing some bare-knuckle body blows to the kidneys can be just the thing.

Remember that another of their vice presidents, Peter, described our Head Honcho as "a roaring lion, seeking whom he may devour" (1 Peter 5:8 BP). Don't miss the full significance of that metaphor, Flambeau. Lions terrify humans. Those who work in our African Division explain that lions can develop an intense taste for human meat. They become man-eaters, and frequently terrorize entire villages.

Peter, you may recall, was speaking of our Chief's power against those who try to live outside of reliance on their CEO (see 1 Peter 5:6–8 BP). The ones who think they can stand in their own strength are our prey. Pain is a devourer. Remember that our CEO Below operates in the territory of the whole earth. Even their vice president John acknowledged that "the whole world" lies in his grasp (1 John 5:19 BP). Through this world he prowls, ready to "swallow up" anyone he encounters—and that's the same swaggering mentality he wants us to adopt.

Ours is a struggle for control, Flambeau, and when our corporate program of deceit fails to deliver, we must shift to a campaign of outright harassment. None of their entities is sacred, none of their individuals off limits. We must use everything at our disposal, up to and including pain, tragedy, misunderstanding, disappointment, and grief.

This brings up another point that I will mention in passing, though we don't dwell on it. All of us feel such enmity against the Competition that it feels so good to hurt the little princes and princesses on whom he has lavished so much attention. This appetite for inflicting harm is difficult to curb. The Competition allows us over the barrier, and we rush in to strike as hard and fast and painfully as we can. Not until later do we ask ourselves why he let us in. It is a hard fact to realize that in this smorgasbord of blood, we don't call the shots. We only reap the side benefits of intimidation that our inflicted pain causes.

These are not things to be spoken of openly, but you need to know at least this much about the way things are. That is all I will say on this subject.

Our Enterprising Founder is the ultimate opportunist, and we must follow in his footsteps to become the takeover barons he wants us to be. We need to exercise daring, tenacity, and cultivate minds like steel traps. Flambeau, you should take an immediate inventory of everything happening in Gene's life, and for that matter, in the lives of each of your clients. Then look for ways to opportunistically use those circumstances to turn them toward acquisitions.

Flambeau Memorandum Twenty-Five

To: hotspur@darkcorp.com
From: flambeau@darkcorp.com
Subject: The Job Factor

So pain is our friend, except when it does us more harm than good? That sounds like more demonic doubletalk. I suppose that there is no way to know whether our use of pain will gather people to our dominion or make them into super ambassadors for the Competition. And for every one of those in the latter category, some poor demon gets skewered.

Whatever we did to Paul, and for some reason no one seems able to tell me what that was, it did not seem to hold him back much. So what, if anything, did the "thorn in the flesh" accomplish?

Here is what I am trying with Gene. I learned from systems analysis that he has a family history of bone and joint weakness. Sure enough, there is some malformation in his knees and elbows. I arranged for the tough ex-Marine to get some inflammation that subjected him to intense pain. I hit both knee and elbow so he won't be able to use a cane to help him. Eventually he'll need to use crutches. I figure that this will force him out of his job, so his dreams for the future will be unattainable. The treatments for the disease are expensive and can have nasty side-effects. He won't be able to find a wife who will want to put up with his aches and pains. So I've covered all of the escape routes toward happiness.

I am not certain why, but I do get such enjoyment from seeing him writhe through the early morning. I find myself not even caring whether he comes back to us if I can sit back and watch the worm turn.

The thing I don't get is, outside of a few minor vetoes, their

CEO has let me do just about anything I can think of. They've been using that communication program they call prayer for him at Glencrest, but I can't see that it's done him any good at all.

It is a truly rewarding experience, and the pain is distracting him from getting as much out of his "Bible study" as he did. I think I have finally hit on the thing that will bring him back, or at least embitter him toward the CEO's Son.

So what do you think? Is this how to use the thorn thing?

Hotspur Memorandum Thirty-Three

To: flambeau@darkcorp.com
From: hotspur@darkcorp.com
Subject: Thorn cushions

At least you are doing something negative, though I still have misgivings. Two aspects of your story give pause. First, you allowed Gene to go to the LCU for prayer. Second, he still is reading the Business Plan daily. These are indicators of faulty execution. You might have waited until we talked a little more about thorns.

Yes, watching them in pain is a great "high," but the important thing is not getting your "jollies" but moving the hurting person and those around them with your intimidation. I still wonder why you haven't managed to yoke this man with one of our female agents. Then, after the commitments are made and they are in the first glow of marital bliss, you could hit Gene with your arthritis program. That is a rather literal application of the "Job's Wife Factor," but it can knock these squirrels right out of their tree. While the man has no personal relationship complicating his life, he just runs for support to the LCU and their Business Plan. That's the last thing you want him to do in his pain.

The fact that you have not been hindered is not a good sign. Watch for a trap.

Let me walk you through this particular aspect of our corporate strategy, since your understanding seems deficient. Then maybe you can make some adjustment to your strategy.

Our CEO Below, while subtle and devious, enjoys inflicting pain as much as the next demon. He likes to inflict it either suddenly and with unforeseen violence or so slowly and subtly that the person doesn't know what has happened until the damage is irreversible. I guess your arthritis idea fits the second scenario.

You'd be surprised how effectively the simplest headache can be at keeping one of these creatures from reading their Business Plan or attending a meeting of the LCU. Intensity isn't the important thing. They can frequently steel themselves for a painful operation, yet be worn down to a nub by ongoing allergies. You may be finding that intense suffering is more rewarding to you, but you already suspect, if I read you correctly, that it is not always as profitable to our larger agenda. If the Job Factor kicks in, we are kicked right out the door.

There are many kinds of pain. Grief brought by the diagnosis of cancer in one's little girl is one of my personal favorites. How these humans squirm when we hurt the ones to whom they give birth.

At the other extreme is the pain we inflict when someone who is supposed to love them does not. This is why having Gene get married before afflicting him might have been a better idea, provided the wife is confirmed in her self-centeredness. Sometimes, admittedly, the Competition really blindsides us with what seemed a sure thing. I'd rather take on Goliath in the ring any day than a wimpy 100-pound woman who is motivated by loyalty to the other side and love for her husband and children.

But there are plenty of successes in family rejection. One example immediately comes to mind, though it did not end well. A young child of two years old was showing signs that his mind was never going to be as good as others. He was a potential burden to his father. So the man poured gasoline on his son and set him ablaze. The family demon assumed that was that, but the boy survived, though he remained badly scarred physically and emotionally, and that didn't help his mental development problems.

No matter. He was still a loser; in fact, he was so anxious to find someone to love him that he acted out his needs with children. So he was placed in one of the human warehouses called prisons. Now he was definitely ours forever.

So why didn't it end well? We had the man in a standard maintenance plan, never dreaming that the Competition would take interest in him—would actually recruit this loser as if he had actual worth. Then he started carrying out simple acts of kindness to fellow inmates and guards. He began showing the mercy of the CEO's Son. He actually tried to make contact with his father to tell him about the CEO, which could have caused us more problems if we hadn't taken out the old man first.

The Competition does that sort of thing all over the world of humans. Their CEO seems to delight in recruiting the most hideous wretches he can find. Then he rations these thorn cushions out to the LCUs. It's almost like a secret office in the LCU that he doesn't tell anyone about, a director of exhibited mercy. Just think about the CEO's Son hiring someone like Paul to be a corporate vice president. Talk about a man with a past, a man with lousy interpersonal skills, and the thorn of pain to boot. But this "least of apostles" turned out to be our worst nightmare.

Be careful that a thorn cushion that has been set down in an LCU doesn't set the whole place on fire against us. I've heard of a weak little country LCU that could not afford a full-time manager. They took a special interest in one family's daughter, who had Downs Syndrome. When she showed an interest in music, she was encouraged and eventually chosen to be the church pianist. People with Downs simply do not learn to play the piano, but this young woman managed, and the LCU only used the songs she could learn to play. The music of that church was terrible, but their grace became known for many miles around. We simply have no countermeasure for that kind of love.

A similar situation occurred at an urban LCU, a church we

thought we had handled when their top manager fell into a sexual affair and abandoned his family. This bunch seemed to be washing down the drain. A couple of splits confirmed that they were headed in the right direction.

What we could not seem to overcome was that their CEO kept placing broken people with thorns in the flesh into that LCU. These thorn cushions somehow inspired and challenged them. One family had a daughter with both autism and severe mental impairment. This girl could be disruptive, and the family might have left in embarrassment at her outbursts. The LCU convinced the parents, though, that nothing was going to change the fact that they and their daughter were part of the church family. The church librarian, a wheelchair-bound woman in constant pain, spent years patiently trying to teach this girl. In fact, she was part of the glue that put the pieces of that group together.

Pain is a mixed bag of thorns? Of course! These people can be fatally damaged goods. We can use their weaknesses against others. We can turn off the people around them with the "If the CEO is good, then why . . . ?" gambit.

Keep in mind, though, that when their CEO takes hold of them for His purposes, you'd better hang on for a very bumpy ride.

To: flambeau@darkcorp.com
From: hotspur@darkcorp.com
Subject: Happier thoughts

When I sent that last e-mail, I noticed that it mostly covered things that go wrong with using humans as thorn cushions. Those are worst-case scenarios. They should not discourage you from using pain. Let's move to a happier subject and focus on garden-variety thorn work.

The human being is a frail creature, so there are innumerable ways in which to inflict pain. You mentioned arthritis, which can be triggered or made more damaging by worries and stress. Anger leads to ulcers and headaches. Even toe stubbing on a chair in the dark can trigger thoughts and words inappropriate for those attached to the Competition. At least they add slapstick for our enjoyment.

Then of course there are the big traumas—auto accidents and physical diseases such as cancer. They intimidate uncooperative clients. For example, suppose Harold is watching Gene's rather fast personal growth. (Yes, I know about his growth.) Harold is considering Gene's invitation to come to the LCU. Then Gene becomes laid up for six months with rheumatoid arthritis that doesn't respond well to treatment.

What should happen, when things are done correctly, is that Harold will think, "If that's what happens to a good guy like Gene, I want nothing to do with this rot." Then if Gene gets mad at the CEO and chucks the whole thing as a result of his illness, we have a double: Gene is back, and Harold is watching Gene come back to us, so he isn't going anywhere.

Some time ago I was responsible for a client who, like your Gene, had become active in one of the Competition's units. He was studying their corporate documents, using prayer, and generally taking a leadership role within the LCU. So one icy day I caused him to slip on his front steps and fracture two bones in his leg. His agony was excruciating, and before long, I had conveyed a negative mindset to him, prompting him to become bitter and resentful.

That opened his mind to other takeover techniques, and soon he became irritated with his colleagues and stopped attending the LCU.

Despite all of its limitations, pain still is our friend—especially when dealing with clients who fail to respond to our more subtle strategic initiatives.

Flambeau Memorandum Twenty-Six

To: hotspur@darkcorp.com
From: flambeau@darkcorp.com
Subject: Strength and weakness

One thing intrigues me about this section, especially given your last communiqué. Their VP admitted that he asked to have this "thorn in the flesh" our CEO Below had sent to afflict him taken away. Apparently when Paul appealed to their CEO to intervene against our Founder's message, the CEO refused and instead raised the subject of grace. Does this have anything to do with why my client's prayers are not being answered?

I must admit I find grace a strange and perplexing concept. I've come across it all over their corporate documents. It seems to have something to do with receiving something undeserved, which flies in the face of everything we hold dear. We want to give these humans exactly what they deserve, from thorns in the flesh to the eternal fires of hell.

Yet their CEO makes such a big deal about justice and righteousness. Taking them into his corporation seems the last thing he would do. Okay, I know he did it anyway. Fine for them. So how can these wretches think they will receive additional undeserved goodies over and above that?

And if he does give them extra gifts, what does grace have to do with the CEO *not intervening* to do what Paul asked? If there was grace to be had, it looks like Paul of all people would have had an "in" for a special favor.

Their VP talked about rejoicing in weakness—how could anyone in his right mind, human or demon, do such a thing? I've been operating from the premise that the only source of anything positive is strength. Then I come across Paul's assertion that, "When I am weak, I am strong." It seems like the antithesis of rational corporate strategy in their world and in ours. From entrepreneur to top executive, success is always based on putting your strength to work. I know their top people consider our Enterprising Founder to be strong—I even came across a reference in Jude 9 of their Business Plan to a dispute between the Head Honcho and their manager of angelic resources. Their top angel wouldn't even launch a verbal assault against our Strong Leader. Instead, he called on his CEO to make the case.

So, in light of this obvious respect they have for our personnel and strategies, how can they possibly place a value on weakness?

Hotspur Memorandum Thirty-Five

To: flambeau@darkcorp.com
From: hotspur@darkcorp.com
Subject: Grace and thorns

You left a few pieces of information out of your last report. I have it on good authority that, because of his illness, Gene is becoming a stronger employee for the Competition. In fact, he has decided to quit his job to go to one of their training institutions, and you couldn't even steer him toward one that is friendly to our corporate message. Some of the other demons connected to Glencrest and its surrounding community have been complaining about Gene's meddling. I also hear that a single nurse in the LCU has been helping Gene deal with his health problems, and they are becoming closer by the day. She is a strong agent of the Competition, recently back from serving in one of their medical units in Central America. This is just the sort of bleeding heart who would be interested in someone like Gene and could help him become a formidable salesperson for the CEO.

Does that about sum up your situation, or are there other disasters I should know about? I have decided that I cannot wait any longer. A committee headed by Drachys of internal demonic affairs will be conducting an independent evaluation of Gene and your other clients. If we don't see a turnaround immediately, you're toast, Flambeau. Or more accurately, you'll become a block of demonic ice on the Siberian tundra. Intimidation—use it or lose everything.

This is just the sort of thing I've been cautioning you about, but instead of improving your strategy, you chose to ignore the warnings. It's one thing to talk about the strategic implications found in 2 Corinthians. It seems to have accomplished nothing other than to make you a better informed foul-up. Let me finish commenting on this section, then you can stew in your own juices until the committee report is finished.

Now, the point of this last section on intimidation.

Paul was allowed an unheard-of dispensation. He was called in to their corporate headquarters for a personal conference in preparation for his work. Then he returned to the human realm. A few of their top managers were scheduled for similar conferences, notably Moses, Isaiah, and Ezekiel. It's the sort of experience that could make a human feel overly impressed with his or her own importance.

Concerned that Paul would be ruined by pride, their CEO decided to permit us to take our best shot at intimidating him with pain. An idiot with the same brain mass as yours jumped on the opportunity, when we should have gone out of our way to lavish authority and easy living on him to take advantage of this potential weakness.

Paul wrote that we had *buffeted* him. I don't recall what we did, if I ever knew. It was a dumb move, unless pressure was exerted from somewhere to do it. In that case it was a great idea that had only some minor drawbacks. The word Paul used means to be beaten or slapped about the face. It was used for the kind of behavior our chief religious agents in Israel carried out toward their CEO-designate when they mocked him, suggested he deserved to die, then spat in his face and beat him, while others struck him with the palms of their hands (Matt. 26:65–67 BP).

You've seen it among these humans, Flambeau. A usually loving mother, prompted by one of us, allows her anger to boil over and belts her toddler in the face. A husband, mistreated by his boss at work, comes home, gets into a shouting match with his wife, and punches or verbally demeans her, usually with just a bit of a nudge from one of our representatives. We always delight in buffeting, either by people or circumstances. Sometimes it can even develop into a pattern of violence the humans will carry on. This is intimidation of the first magnitude, which leads to discouragement, disillusionment, and maybe even to reacquisition.

One of their corporate values is to persevere (Luke 18:1; Gal. 6:9 BP). The more intensely and steadily we buffet our clients, the greater the chances of our acquiring control over them, and the less likely they are to persevere in growth. After a due evaluation of your client, you must leverage the asset of pain into intimidation and discouragement.

Remember how our Top Guy Down Below used people as intimidators. Our agents Hymenaeus and Philetus were intimidators against Paul and at least somewhat effective (2 Tim. 2:17 BP). Alexander the coppersmith caused him great harm (4:14). Elymas the Sorcerer was honored for his use of intimidation by being called a son of our CEO (Acts 13:8 BP). We want to convey an intimidating message: "Any who dare resist our message will be chewed up by lion-like tactics." It's time for a scorched-earth policy when it comes to letting them get away with things, and your meek, mild, distinctively undemonic approach to your clients can no longer be permitted.

We've had some discussion about how the CEO Below stripped one of their early pioneers, Job. Shrewd devil that he is, our Top Guy took everything from Job except for his carping, complaining wife. I've already pointed out that the intimidation was more against her than it was her husband. She became our messenger, reinforcing the message that the only logical response to a devastating crisis is to curse their Founder and die (Job 2:9 BP).

Then the Guy Down Below inserted a group of comforters who gave an analysis of Job's situation that dripped with worldly sophistication and wise philosophy. They dumped a trainload of guilt-inducing charges, assuming that anyone with as many problems as Job must have committed a serious crime (see, for example, Job 4:7 BP).

Job's comforters provided a sterling example of how we can use people to convey the message of intimidation. In this case, we virtually turned the Competition's message against them, pointing out how the only logical conclusion Job should consider was that he had some hidden personal failure.

Granted, the Competition's CEO had pinpointed a hidden weakness in Job's character—a great fear that some disaster would befall him or his family (Job 3:25 BP). But we were able to bring out a number of other character traits, such as bitterness, suicidal depression, agitation, and even anger toward the CEO. We might have found more had the CEO Himself not intervened. We evidently had stepped across some hidden boundary line, beyond which we could not go in playing with Job's mind.

There's a lot you could learn about the finer points of intimidation from the job our CEO did with Job.

When we inflict thorns, we must be careful to confuse their purpose. This usually isn't too difficult, since we aren't normally told why we are allowed an opportunity to attack. Sometimes suffering is punishment or discipline (as in Heb. 12:7–13 BP), and sometimes it serves other corporate purposes (12:3 BP). In the Competition's value system, getting slapped around in discipline is not just punishment. Sometimes they use it for preparation, like the humans' military boot camp system. It builds them into something less desirable to us (Rom. 5:1–5 BP). This seems part of what's happening to Gene now.

And you thought it was your great idea.

In a situation where pain is being used for growth, we must circumvent the process by confusing the person on the spot. If pain has a punishment aspect, their CEO is just being unfair. If pain is His's growth through discipline tool, obviously the person, like Job, must have done something evil to get "a board up the side of the head." You can even convince the fool that suffering makes service to their CEO impossible, when their purpose in it is actually to make the person fit to serve.

This matter of grace is a dangerous concept, Flambeau. It's a key component to their corporate message, one that plays a central role in their Business Plan. They use this term to mean undeserved favor (as in Romans 5:2; Ephesians 2:8). And in a way that we cannot figure out, the undeserved merit that brings salvation becomes the preserving and energizing power that enables these humans to be so frustratingly resilient when we throw our worst at them. It is this power for resilience that is meant when their CEO told Paul, "My grace is sufficient." *Sufficient* here means adequate to ward off danger.

Don't miss the implication of that sufficiency; it's a dangerous concept for us. It runs totally counter to our message of intimidation through pain. Anyone who understands the sufficiency of the power can walk through the lion's den without feeling any fear or intimidation. From our standpoint, the whole point of suffering is destroyed if they think they have some mysterious force that can keep them from being consumed by His Debased Majesty.

I want you to think back over the tactics we've talked about. When it comes down to it, they all are only useful if they can confuse this message of grace.

This insane corporate message of grace ultimately frustrates our designs, because it allows them to remain contented. Their literature presents contentment as a major corporate value (Phil. 4:11 BP). That's why we can't allow contentment. We simply must not stand by and permit anyone—whether a vice president like Paul, or the lowest, least significant member of one of their local competition units, to adopt the attitude that says, as Paul did, "I take pleasure in infirmities, in reproaches, in needs, in persecutions, in distresses" (2 Cor. 12:10 BP). That kind of thinking, along with the strange notion that "when I am weak, then I am strong" is among their most dangerous of all thought patterns.

We may consider it insane. It may seem to make them vulnerable. But the truth is quite to the contrary, Flambeau. When they start thinking that way, instead of depending on their own resources, they tap into sufficient grace, this unusual source of energy their Founder makes available. They become practically immune to our efforts and ever more entrenched in their corporation's message.

And that's where you've gotten yourself into trouble, Flambeau. You believed that, because their vice president was under attack, he was in fact weak. It was not so for Paul—or for your client Gene.